A MIDSUMMER NIGHT'S SCREAM

R. L. STINE

SQUARE
FISH

FEIWEL AND FRIENDS
NEW YORK

SQUARE
FISH

An Imprint of Macmillan
175 Fifth Avenue
New York, NY 10010
macteenbooks.com

Square Fish and the Square Fish logo are trademarks of Macmillan and
are used by Feiwel & Friends under license from Macmillan.

Square Fish books may be purchased for business or promotional use.
For information on bulk purchases, please contact the Macmillan
Corporate and Premium Sales Department at (800) 221-7945 x5442
or by e-mail at specialmarkets@macmillan.com.

Library of Congress Cataloging-in-Publication Data Available

ISBN 978-1-250-04434-1 (paperback) / ISBN 978-1-250-04244-6 (e-book)

Originally published in the United States by Feiwel & Friends
First Square Fish Edition: 2014
Book designed by Ashley Halsey
Square Fish logo designed by Filomena Tuosto

10 9 8 7 6 5 4 3 2 1

LEXILE: 470L

PART ONE

The course of true love never did run smooth;
But either it was different in blood . . .

—William Shakespeare,
A Midsummer Night's Dream

1

ONE NIGHT IN THE WOODS

ONE HAND ON THE WHEEL, one hand around Darlene's shoulders, Tony pounded the gas pedal, and the van roared over the bumps and pits of the narrow dirt road. Leaning against the window on Darlene's right, Sue gritted her teeth and absorbed every jolt and jerk in silence. Tony was driving too fast, trying to impress Darlene, and Sue had to fight down her fear.

The van was roaring through thick woods, and the over-hanging trees blocked the evening light, making Sue feel as if the world had gone black-and-white.

In the backseat, Randy, Brian, and Cindy were singing a children's song, "Teddy Bear's Picnic." Singing and laughing at the same time. Darlene shook her head. Sue covered her ears.

Sue was the shy one in the group of friends. She appeared on edge with them, as if she'd love to be somewhere else.

The van hit a big stone, and the six kids flew up from their seats, their heads thumping the ceiling. The wheel spun wildly in Tony's hand. Sue and Cindy screamed as they veered toward the trees. Laughing, Tony swung the car back onto the road.

"Man, this van can really rock and roll," Randy said from the backseat.

"Like really," Tony said. He tightened his arm around Darlene, pulling her closer.

Sue gripped her door handle tightly. She frowned at Tony. It was obvious she wished Tony would stop trying to wow Darlene and drive a little slower. The sky had grown even darker.

Cindy sat between Brian and Randy in the back. She was sweet-looking, with wavy blond hair down to her shoulders. She wore a ruffled peasant blouse that showed plenty of skin. Randy had short blond hair and looked about twelve, even with the cigarette dangling from his mouth.

Darlene was smoking, too. She had a dark ponytail, her hair mostly hidden under a polka-dot bandanna. The bandanna flapped in the wind from Tony's open window. Darlene always wore the same black leather jacket and black denim jeans. She liked to look tough.

Tony's dark hair was ruffled by the wind as the van sped through the trees. He had a lean, serious face, but his eyes crinkled at the sides, as if he were always enjoying a private joke.

"How about some music?" Randy asked.

Tony uttered an annoyed sigh. "I already told you, the radio is busted. This is my cousin's van and—"

That's when the car hit something in the road and spun rapidly out of control. Jerked to one side, the six teens heard a hard *thud* and then the clang of metal against rock.

"Whoooaaaa!" Tony uttered a wide-eyed cry.

The car lurched forward, then shot back hard with a squeal. Silence.

Sue gazed out the window, her face revealing her fear. "Did we hit a deer?"

"Just a rock," Tony said, and then added, "I think."

The three in the backseat sat in stunned silence.

Tony tried to gun the engine. Nothing. He turned the key in the ignition, but the van refused to respond.

"Come on. Come on. Go!" It was easy to see that Tony was the most impatient of the group. No—impatient wasn't the right word. He was hot-headed, ready to explode for any reason.

Several more tries to start the van. Sue shut her eyes. Darlene tapped the dashboard nervously.

"Go go go," Randy urged the van from the backseat.

They were deep in the woods in the middle of nowhere. It was miles to the lake lodge where they were heading.

Tony let out an exasperated cry. He slammed the wheel with both hands. "I don't believe this."

He shoved open the driver's door and jumped outside. Everyone started talking at once. The air in the van grew steamy and hot. They all piled out.

Tall trees rose up on both sides of the narrow dirt road.

Brian put a hand on Sue's shoulder. "Hey, Sue, we'll be okay."

Sue forced a smile, but everyone could see her trembling.

"Nice night for a walk," Darlene said, rolling her eyes. "I love walking miles and miles in a dark forest, don't you?"

No one answered her.

Tony was peering under the hood. He slammed his fist on the fender and cursed. "Too dark. I can't see a thing."

"Since when do you know how to fix a car?" Randy said.

"Since when do I need *your* opinion?" Tony shot back. He bumped up against Randy, fists clenched.

Randy raised both hands in surrender and backed off.

The discussion of what to do didn't take long. Stay overnight in the van? Or walk and try to find a house or cabin with someone who could help them start it up again? The unanimous decision was to look for help.

And so they left everything in the van and, huddling close together, started off along the path through the trees. The only sounds were the soft thuds of their shoes on the dirt and the endless shrill chirp of crickets all around.

"What kind of a nut would live in the middle of a forest?" Darlene complained. "We'll be walking forever."

"Unless we're attacked by wolves," Randy joked.

"Not funny, man." Tony moved to confront Randy again. Randy raised his hands in surrender and backed off.

"There may be a bigger road or a highway up ahead," Cindy said. She was the optimist in the group.

How long did they crunch through the trees? An hour? More? It was hard to keep track of the time. Tony kept his arm around Darlene as they led the way. Brian was big and brawny. He kept mopping sweat off his forehead with the back of his hand as he trudged along.

Cindy was the first to cry out. "Wow! Look."

The house came into view, black against the charcoal sky, as if it had magically popped up from nowhere.

Sue gasped in surprise and squeezed Brian's hand. The six friends stared at the house, rising like a dark fortress in front of them.

"Welcome to Dracula's Castle," Darlene murmured.

It did look more like a castle than a house. Dark towers rose up on both sides of a long sloping roof. Were those *bats* flapping in the evening sky, circling the twin towers?

They trotted toward the house eagerly, although it didn't appear inviting. No lights. The windows were as dark as the night, and as the six teens drew nearer, they could see that bars covered every one.

"Looks like a prison," Randy muttered.

"Who would live in a creepy place like this?" Darlene asked.

"A rich person," Tony said. "A rich person who will help us get going again."

"Maybe a rich person who doesn't want any guests," Brian said.

But pounding on the tall, wooden slab of a front door didn't bring anyone to open it. Tony ran along the side of the house, peering into the barred windows. "I don't think anyone is home," he reported.

"Hey, look," Darlene called to him. "The door..."

She pushed the thick door open. Everyone stepped up behind Darlene. She crept over the threshold. "Anyone home? Hey—anyone here?" She had a sharp, tough voice. She sounded hard, even when she was trying to be sweet.

No reply.

A few seconds later, they stood in the front entryway. Sue fumbled on the wall, found a light switch, and clicked it. She uttered a cry of surprise as bright ceiling lights flashed on high above their heads.

"Nice!" Tony declared, gazing around. Beyond the hall stood a huge front room, filled with old-fashioned armchairs and couches.

Darlene shook her head. "Is this the Ritz? The guy who owns this place has got to be a millionaire!"

"Anyone here?" Randy shouted. His voice rang through the empty rooms.

They moved through the front room, into a large library with floor-to-ceiling bookshelves, through another hallway, into a long dining room, turning on lights as they went.

Cindy tossed back her blond hair and squinted down the length of the oak dining-room table. "This room... it's bigger than the lunchroom at school," she stammered. She slid out a heavy, tall-backed chair and sat down at the table. "Somebody serve me dinner. I'll have pheasant under glass."

Sue raised her eyes to the ceiling. She was surprised to

see two old-fashioned-looking swords—like pirate swords—crisscrossed high above the table. They were suspended in the air on thin cords, halfway between the table and the high ceiling.

"Far out," she murmured. "This is the strangest house. Why are those swords over the table?" She pulled out a chair and sat down next to Cindy.

Darlene and Tony lingered near the door. They wrapped their arms around each other. Tony pressed Darlene against the wall. Darlene held the back of Tony's head with both hands and kissed him and kissed him, long wet kisses.

"Hey, break it up, sex maniacs," Randy called to them. "Did you forget we're not moving in here? We came to find help, remember?"

Tony edged Darlene out of his way and came storming toward Randy. "I'm tired of you being in my business," he growled. "You've been on my back the whole trip."

Randy didn't retreat this time. "Man, I don't know what your problem is. I was just saying—"

He didn't get to finish. Tony took a swing at him.

Randy ducked and the punch sailed over his head. "Hey, cool it, man. We have to—"

The others cried out as Tony's next punch caught Randy in the pit of his stomach. Brian dove forward to pull Tony back.

Randy folded up, grabbing his middle and groaning. He staggered back into the long serving cabinet. The impact of his body against the dark wood cabinet sent it thudding into the wall.

A shadow moved over the dining-room table. Overhead, the dangling swords started to swing. One of them slipped from its cord and sailed straight down.

Cindy opened her mouth in a shrill squeal. "Noooooo!"

The sword came slicing down.

They all heard a *squisssh*.

Cindy's scream cut off with a gurgle.

"Oh my god. Oh my god!" Sue shrieked. The room rang with shrill cries of horror.

Eyes bulging, Cindy raised a bloody stump. Her hand had been cut off cleanly at the wrist. It sat in front of her on the tabletop, thumb and fingers outstretched. Like a small white crab.

2

ANOTHER ACCIDENT?

"OH MY GOD ... OH MY GOD ..."

Bright-red blood began to spurt from Cindy's open wrist. It squirted high in the air, splashing onto the table.

Cindy screamed and screamed, waving the stump in front of her. Sue turned and tried to hug her. Blood splattered the front of her skirt and top.

Grunting and groaning like a hurt animal, Cindy toppled off the chair and collapsed to the floor. Silent now, she didn't move.

The others rushed to her. Only Darlene held back, her face suddenly pale, her features tight with fear. "Get something to wrap around her arm," Tony said. "We have to stop the bleeding."

"Too late," Sue told him. She was on her knees, leaning over Cindy. Cindy's eyes were wide and glassy. Her mouth hung open. She wasn't breathing. "Too late. I ... I think she's dead."

"Noooo!" The cries rang through the enormous room. "She can't be!"

"Oh my god. No. Please, no."

"We have to get help," Randy said. "We've got to call the police. Call an ambulance."

"There has to be a phone," Brian said. "Did anyone see a phone?"

"Maybe in the kitchen?" Sue suggested. Cindy's blood was darkening on the front of Sue's clothes.

They stumbled to the kitchen door at the far end of the dining room. Tony got there first. "Yes!" he cried. "A wall phone."

He lifted the receiver and put it to his ear. His face appeared to collapse. "No dial tone. It's dead." He studied the phone. "Hey—the cord has been cut!"

They all stared at the dangling phone cord.

"S-someone doesn't want us to call for help," Darlene choked out. She swallowed hard. "Th-that sword that dropped on Cindy's hand—maybe it wasn't an accident. Maybe someone *dropped* the sword on her. What if the killer is still in the house?"

"That's crazy!" Tony cried. "Don't talk crazy ideas. Keep it calm, hear? It *had* to be an accident."

"We have to do *something*," Darlene whispered. She lit a cigarette with a trembling hand. "We can't stay in here arguing with each other. There's a dead body in the dining room. There has to be a way to reach the police."

Tony pointed to the kitchen window, thick bars outside the glass like all the other windows. "Very dark out there," he said. "And nothing but woods for miles. I don't want to go out till morning."

"I . . . I really don't like this," Sue stammered. Her whole body trembled.

"Who does?" Darlene said, taking a deep drag of her cigarette.

Tony walked over and put his arms around her. She lowered her head to his shoulder.

"We need to think," Randy said. "I'm like in shock. It's hard to think straight." He rubbed the front of his t-shirt. "Maybe it's because I'm starving."

"I'm hungry, too," Brian said. "We haven't eaten anything since this morning, and—"

"How can you think about food when Cindy is lying in there dead?" Sue demanded. She wrapped her arms around her chest as if shielding herself from danger.

Brian put a hand on her shoulder. "I think Randy is right. We'll all think more clearly if we have something to eat."

"Who says there's any food in this creepy old house?" Tony asked, scowling at Randy.

Randy shrugged. "We can look—can't we?"

He bent down and started sliding kitchen drawers open. Tony moved quickly across the kitchen. He grabbed Randy by the shoulders and tried to pull him back. "Don't touch anything, Randy. What if Darlene is right? This whole house could be a trap. We can't just make sandwiches and pretend we're not in danger."

Randy pulled free of Tony. He tugged open another

cabinet door. "But I'm hungry, man. And when I'm hungry, I'm hungry."

"We're all hungry," Brian said. "Tony, we'll think better if we grab a bite. We'll be able to make a plan."

"I don't like this," Darlene said. "We need to plan how to protect ourselves in case—"

"Found something!" Randy shouted. He pulled out a loaf of bread. He raised it for the others to see. He turned to the counter. "Look. A toaster. I'll make toast. See what's in the fridge. Any butter? Jelly?"

He walked toward a silver toaster on the counter. Tony blocked his path. "I'm warning you, man . . ."

"And I'm warning *you*, man," Randy grunted. They had a short staring contest.

Finally, Tony backed off. "Okay, whatever you say. Make your toast."

Randy slid two slices of bread into the toaster. He started to push the lever down.

He gasped at the loud, electronic buzz. A bright flash of light burst from the toaster.

Darlene let out a shriek. Sue and Brian stumbled back against the counter.

Randy's whole body jerked wildly as a jagged bolt of white electricity crackled up his arm, then around his shoulder and head.

The electricity roared as it swept over him. Randy's body jolted and thrashed. He opened his mouth in a shriek of pain and horror. But his cry was drowned out by the crackling, roaring electrical charge from the toaster.

3

A BAD FALL

THE WHITE-HOT JAGGED BOLTS OF current shot around his head, his shoulders, his whole body. Randy's face started to burn. The roar of the powerful jolts grew deafening.

His arms flew straight up. Trapped inside the burning, crackling power charges, Randy started to do a wild dance. His arms swung above his head. His legs bent and kicked. The pain of the electrical jolts forced him to dance . . . dance . . .

Then his screams stopped. His eyes closed. His head tilted back at an impossible angle. His eyes bulged, staring blankly at the ceiling.

The others gaped in helpless horror. They knew Randy was dead. The electrical shock had killed him. But it kept him dancing. Jolt after jolt. His arms flailing, his legs bobbing and bending. A crazy, horrifying dance.

A dance of the dead.

Finally, he collapsed to the floor.

He didn't move. Darlene's sobs broke the silence. Tony moved to hold her, but she knelt down beside Randy and held him by the shoulders. His mouth hung open. His face was burned black.

Tony banged his fists on the wall angrily. Brian stared wide-eyed, as if he'd gone into a trance.

"I warned him. You heard me," Tony said. "You all heard me." He was trying to sound tough, but his voice cracked.

"Too late for warnings," Sue murmured.

"We've got to get it together," Tony said, shaking his head. "We've got to think. Think . . ."

"We've got to get out of this house before . . . before some-one kills us all," Brian said.

Darlene set Randy's charred head down gently. Then she climbed to her feet. "Brian is right. Let's go. Let's just get out."

She spun toward the kitchen door and strode over to it. Sue watched her struggle with the door handle. "Locked," Darlene reported. "We're locked in."

"Try the front door," Sue said. She led the way back through the dining room. Past Cindy dead on the floor, her pale hand still sitting on the table. Through the library and front room. Back to the tall front door.

Tony grabbed the door handle. Pushed, then pulled. Angrily, he set his shoulder against it and tried to force it.

"Locked," he finally admitted, breathing hard. "Someone must have locked it. We're . . . trapped in here."

"Who is doing this to us?" Brian cried, pressing his

hands to the sides of his face. "What crazy maniac wants to kill us all?"

Tony frowned at Brian. "Get it together, man. If you lose your cool now, you'll never get out of here."

"But . . . but . . ." Brian sputtered. "The doors are locked and the windows are barred."

"Upstairs," Darlene said. "Maybe we can climb out an upstairs window."

Their shoes thudded on the hardwood floors as they made their way to the bottom of a steep stairway. The four teens gazed up into the darkness at the top. They hesitated.

"Are you sure you want to go up there?" Brian asked. "It's so dark, man."

"We have no choice," Darlene said, pushing the two boys aside, "if we want to get out of this house alive." She raised her foot to the first step. "Follow me."

They watched her run quickly up the wooden stairs. They were steep. There was no banister. And each step squeaked when she climbed onto it.

She turned back to the three at the bottom. "What are you waiting for? Come on!"

She raised her shoe to the next stair—and stumbled. They all screamed as Darlene fell. There was no step beneath her. The top boards were missing. It was an open hole.

Darlene uttered a shrill wail as her body sank into the hole. She fell quickly. She raised her arms to stop herself, but she wasn't quick enough. Her scream was cut off by a sickening *craaack*.

The sound of her neck breaking.

Her eyes went wide. Her face froze. Her body plummeted into the hole, and on the way down, her chin caught the stair edge. The fall broke her neck—and she died instantly.

At the bottom of the stairs, Tony and Brian were screaming, staring up at Darlene's head.

Sue turned away from the scene of horror. She pointed at a strange man who suddenly appeared behind them. He was very short and had a wild nest of black hair on his head and a heavy black beard that cast his face in shadow.

"Stop it!" Sue shrieked at him. "Why don't you *stop* it? Stop it! *Stop it!*"

4

CURSED

THE MOVIE SCREEN WENT WHITE. My friend Delia Jacobs and I sat staring at it, blinking at the sudden bright light. I tried to swallow but my throat was too dry.

"That . . . was so horrible," I said in a whisper. I pressed my hands against my cheeks. My palms felt cold and wet against my hot face. I could feel the blood pulsing at my temples.

"Claire, I totally don't believe it," Delia said. "But it really happened, didn't it? Those poor kids. Trying to make a movie and . . . and . . ." Her voice faded.

Delia gripped the arms of the leather chair. She shuddered. "We actually watched those three young actors die. I think I'm going to be sick. Really."

"Me, too."

We were sitting in the front row of my family's basement screening room. It's a pretty awesome room—six rows of soft, comfortable chairs, a huge LED screen, a theater-quality sound system, and in the corner, an antique popcorn cart on two wheels that actually makes the best popcorn ever.

But we didn't make popcorn today. Delia and I knew what we were going to watch was truly horrifying. And real.

My dad begged us not to watch it. He said it would give us nightmares. "I know you're curious," he said. "But sometimes it's better not to know the reality."

Dad is an avoider. He likes to see the bright side of things. He has a way of pushing aside the unpleasant. I'm a lot like him. But this time I didn't agree.

Delia and I decided we had to see that film. We had to know what we were getting involved in.

Let me explain.

Delia and I have always dreamed about acting in movies, and our dream has come true. This summer we are going to be in the remake of *Mayhem Manor*. That's why we just sat through the original *Mayhem Manor* film from 1960.

Or, at least, what exists of it.

The film ended when Darlene fell into that open stair and broke her neck. That was the last scene they shot. Because of the three horrible accidents—and the three deaths—the movie was never finished.

It was a horror movie that turned into real horror.

Three young actors lost their lives while the camera rolled. Books have been written about the tragic accidents that stopped the film. Some people believed that Mayhem Manor was *cursed*. It became a dark Hollywood legend.

My mom and dad run WoodCast Studios in Burbank. They make one or two movies a year. Dad decided to green-light a new version of the old horror film. Sixty years had passed since the original *Mayhem Manor*. He knew a remake of a cursed film would get a lot of press, a lot of attention.

Delia and I were desperate to be in it. As I said, we both totally want to be actors. We both auditioned . . .

. . . and the rest is movie history.

Okay, okay. I exaggerate. But, you never know.

"Did you watch it?" A voice from behind us. My dad walked to the front of the screening room.

"Yeah. We did," I said. "Where were you? You were going to watch it with us."

He shrugged. He looked tired. "We had a problem on the set of *Please Don't*, that comedy we're doing. So what else is new? I had to stay late."

I told you Dad is an avoider. I knew he wouldn't watch it with us.

He rubbed his smooth cheeks. "I owe you girls an apology. I should never have given you the footage. It's too up-setting and—"

"Too late," Delia murmured. "My stomach is already acting like a wave machine at Six Flags."

"I know I'm going to have nightmares tonight," I said.

"I warned you," Dad said. "Maybe if you keep telling yourself it happened sixty years ago . . ."

"How did it happen?" Delia asked. She suddenly looked very pale. "Did someone like deliberately kill those actors?"

Dad shook his head. "It was a big mystery. A mystery that was never really solved. The L.A. police . . . the FBI . . . private investigators . . . they all decided the deaths were accidental. Three horrible accidents."

My stomach churned again. "I feel sick. Really."

"I'm so sorry," Dad said. "But I guess you have to know the truth. You're going back into that house to film our remake. So you need to know what happened there."

Delia and I gazed at the blank screen on the wall. I kept hearing those awful screams in my ears. Not acting. Real screams.

"If either of you wants to quit . . ." Dad started.

"No way!" Delia and I said in unison.

"You're right. We have to keep telling ourselves it was sixty years ago," Delia said. "It's history, right?" She was trying to be positive, but her voice trembled.

"We're *so psyched* to be in this movie," I said. "We've both waited so long. It's our dream, you know. We can't wait to start. Right, Delia?"

Delia nodded. "Can't wait."

It's true. I couldn't wait for rehearsals to start. My first movie. What could be more exciting?

Now if only I could get those three kids to stop screaming in my ears.

PART TWO

5

STRANGE IMPULSES

A WEEK AFTER DELIA AND I watched the footage of the old film, I went to Ross Harper's party hoping to find Jake Castellano. Like the song says, *I had lovin' on my mind.*

Ross lives in an enormous mansion with a swimming pool the size of Lake Tahoe, on Loma Vista in Beverly Hills, which is a short drive from my house. Of course, my dad had to drive Delia and me to the party because of the screwed-up California driving laws.

Delia and I are almost seventeen, which means we can drive anywhere we want to—until curfew time at eleven at night. Which makes no sense. How are we supposed to get home if we can't drive after eleven? I mean, a lot of my friends don't go *out* till eleven.

Hey, but no complaints from me. Any pool party at Ross's house is worth *walking* to, especially if his parents are away.

Delia sat in the backseat of Dad's BMW. She had her

phone in one hand and drummed her fingers on the seat with the other. I could hear the tinny beats of music escaping from the earbuds in her ears.

Did I mention that Delia and I are like *this* (two fingers close together)? I don't think you could call her my BFF, but she's definitely my Best Friend For Now.

That's because her mother keeps talking about leaving L.A., getting away from the lunatics, she says. Mrs. Jacobs and her new boyfriend aren't in the movie business, and if you don't work in movies in L.A., where are you?

Delia doesn't get along with either of them. The new boyfriend grooms dogs at home, and Delia hates dogs because she is allergic to all the fur. So she sleeps at my house whenever she can. Actually, she *lives* at my house and just goes home to change her clothes.

Dad seemed preoccupied as he drove. He kept his eyes on the twisting road and crinkled his face, as if he had unpleasant thoughts running through his mind. I guessed he was thinking about going back to work tomorrow.

I didn't want to think about movies tonight. I wanted to think about Ross Harper's party. His parties can be way wild.

When Ross's parents are away, some kids get pretty messed up, mostly on beer and wine and smoking things. And we all know why couples slink off to the pool house across the terrace. You don't need to guess. I mean, it's a *three-bedroom* pool house!

Well, tonight I wanted to find Jake Castellano and get him alone somehow, away from Shawn O'Reilly, his hulking shadow, and just spill my guts. Tell him how I feel about him. The whole sweaty hands, heart-fluttering thing.

Oh, wow. I don't want to be living some douchy kind of teen romance. But I wouldn't mind *some* romance. With Jake, that is. We've been bumping up against each other most of our lives, so he thinks of me as—wait for it—a *friend*. Is that the *worst* word in the English language?

Delia didn't want to come along. She doesn't like Ross Harper. Delia says she hates rich people like Ross.

Delia's father made piles of money in real estate in the Valley. But I guess that doesn't count to her since he ran off with some kind of countess and left her and her mother in their house on Melrose.

When I told Delia that Shawn would probably be at the party, her dark eyes flashed and her whole expression changed. She's been crushing on Shawn for weeks now. She says he hasn't noticed. Which means Shawn is basically plant life, because Delia is the hottest girl at Beverly Hills Academy. Ask anyone.

I don't really understand what she sees in Shawn. He's a big goofy teddy bear. And my idea of a good time isn't hanging out at the beach, watching Shawn draped over a board in his wet suit, waiting for the next good wave.

Anyway, my dad dropped us off at the gate in front of Ross's house. Yes, there's a tall iron fence around the property. Through the bars of the gate, I gazed up at the house, bathed in white light.

I pressed the button on the intercom. The gate buzzed

and started to swing open. As Delia and I walked up the wide driveway, we could hear music and kids talking and laughing around the pool on the other side of the house.

It was a perfect L.A. night. The air was soft and warm and smelled sweet from the hibiscus beds along the drive. The huge house glowed. Like a movie set, I thought.

As a maid showed us through the house to the terrace in back, I felt kind of tingly. You know. Like this could be an important party.

Was I tense much? You think?

Well, I'd had Jake on my mind all day. Crazy. He was like furniture. I mean, he'd been in my life forever. Our families are so close. Our parents are business partners—they run the WoodCast movie studio together—and we live next door to each other.

I'm not sure when I started to think about Jake differently. But I was *definitely* thinking about him. And tonight . . .

Who knew what tonight would bring?

Do I have to describe the party scene to you? You've seen parties, right? Maybe not on a terrace as big as the Burbank airport. I saw at least two dozen kids around the pool, mostly from our school, but a few I didn't recognize.

They were standing in small groups or sprawled on the white wicker pool chairs, beer bottles in their hands, so I figured Ross's parents weren't home. Kids were talking loudly over the dance music that boomed from the speakers on poles around the pool.

Some kids were in the blue sparkly water, mostly standing

in the shallow end with their drinks on the edge of the deck. I waved to Ross, who had his arm around a tall red-headed girl I'd never seen before. I didn't see Jake or Shawn.

Delia had a short blue-and-white camisole shift over her swimsuit. She just pulled it off and tossed it over a chair. She kicked off her sandals and slid them under the chair. She has a great body, and I actually saw heads turn to stare at her as she made her way to the others, rocking her blue bikini.

I wore white tennis shorts and a tank top. I didn't plan to swim tonight. Hey, I'm all right in a bikini. I'm not a total knockout like Delia, but I'm okay in a cute way. Some people say I look like Cameron Diaz. But, you know, younger. Not so slutty.

Couples were dancing on the side of the deck. They had green and blue lightsticks raised above their heads and they were jumping to the throbbing beats, like a crazy rave.

I stepped close to the pool and actually gasped when I saw Annalee Franklin doing slow laps in the clear water. I gasped because I thought she was *totally naked*.

That would be bold, even for Annalee. But as she swam closer, I saw her bikini. It was two strings. Literally. Two strings.

She gazed up at me with her green cat-eyes. She probably saw my mouth hanging open. "Hey, Claire," she called, paddling gently, water running off her smooth black hair. "Shooting starts tomorrow. We're going to be seeing a lot more of each other."

"I'm seeing a *lot* of you now!" I replied. I knew she couldn't hear me over the music and the splash of the water. Annalee's mother was some kind of beauty queen in China before the family moved here. And Annalee has the same perfect skin, cheekbones to die for, and fabulous smile.

"I'll be seeing you on the set," she said. She ducked under the surface, then resumed her slow swim. Were kids along the deck staring at her? Duh.

"Don't judge her," a voice said. I turned to see Delia grinning at me.

"Don't judge her?"

"She's needy," Delia said.

"For sure. She *needs* a swimsuit," I said.

Delia gave me a shove. "Prude."

That kind of stunned me. "Huh? Really? Am I a prude?"

But Delia took off without answering. I raised my eyes and saw where she was hurrying. Shawn and Jake had just stepped out from the house.

My mouth suddenly felt dry. I watched Delia run up to the two guys as I crossed to the wet bar at the other end of the pool. Ross turned to greet me with a glass in his hand. "Hey." We slapped knuckles. "Claire, what are you drinking?"

"Nothing yet," I said. I nodded at the glass in his hand. "What's that?"

"Red Bull and Stoli."

I blinked. "Any good?"

He handed it to me. I took a sip. Awful.

I grabbed a Diet Coke and tapped the can against his glass, like we were toasting. I took a long drink.

Ross and I were kind of a couple for about an hour in tenth grade. But he decided it was more fun to play *World of Warcraft* with his buddies and get wrecked from his parents' liquor cabinet than hang with me.

No big whoop.

"When is your birthday party?" Ross asked. "Some kids were talking about it."

"June twenty-first," I said. "That's the summer solstice. Midsummer night. It's going to be crazy huge. At the movie studio. That's the longest night of the year, and the party's going to rock all night. Are you going to be in town?"

He shrugged. "Hope so." He took a long drink. Some of it spilled down his chin. "I hear you're in that ... that horror movie."

I nodded. "Yeah. Delia, too. And Annalee. And Jake is working as a PA or something. I'm so excited. My parents finally gave in and said I could be in a movie. We've been rehearsing. We start filming this week."

He raised his eyes to me. "Aren't you scared? Filming in that haunted house?"

I opened my mouth to answer, but he waved to someone and took off toward the pool. I took another long drink from the Coke can.

Claire, you came to this party to talk to Jake, and you're going to do it.

I turned to go find him. The billowing light from the pool made the whole terrace shimmer blue and white. Kind of magical. Like we were all underwater.

"Think fast!"

The cry made me duck, and a red Nerf football sailed over my head. It bounced once on the deck, then splashed into the pool.

Jake ran up, laughing, and grabbed me by the shoulders.

Is he going to kiss me?

Of course not. What was I thinking?

"Nice catch," he said.

I grinned back at him. "Were you trying to knock me into the pool?"

He nodded. "Maybe."

"Thanks."

"Don't mention it."

This was a thrilling conversation.

Jake is tall and good-looking, with a slender, serious face, unbrushed brown hair, blue eyes, and a knockout smile. He's one of these guys—you know the type—who breeze through life and never seem to be trying too hard.

I swallowed hard. *Courage time, Claire.* We were standing right under a music speaker. I took his arm and led him past the jumping couples with their flashing lightsticks, toward the pool house. "I . . . wanted to talk to you."

That wasn't the swimming pool pump pounding like that. That was my heart beating.

"Hey, I wanted to talk to you, too," he said.

Wow.

"You go first," I said.

"No. You."

"No. You." I shoved him. "Go ahead. What do you want to talk about?"

"Well . . ." We stood in the shadow of the pool house wall. He glanced back toward the crowd. "You see . . . I just wondered . . ."

This was definitely weird. Jake and I never had trouble talking to each other. We were like brother and sister, right?

"Yes? Spit it out, Jake."

"I wondered if Delia ever mentions me. I mean—"

"You *what*?" I kind of lost it there. I squeaked the words.

"I think Delia likes me," Jake said. "But I don't really catch any signals. Know what I mean? I mean, she's so totally *smoking*. You and she are like best friends. So I just wondered . . . Does she talk about me at all?"

Whoa. I replied through clenched teeth. "Why don't you ask Delia yourself?"

His eyes went wide. He saw that I was pissed off. "Is . . . is there a problem here?"

"No," I insisted. "How could there be a problem?"

He gazed at me for a long moment. Then he shrugged, as if dismissing the whole conversation. "What did *you* want to tell *me*, Claire?"

"Uh . . . nothing. Just . . . I'll see you at the studio. You're a PA on the set, right?"

"I'm supposed to be an intern. For Zack Fox, the film editor." His sandy brown hair fell over his forehead. I wanted to brush it back with my hand. Suddenly, his expression changed. "But I'm thinking maybe I'll quit."

"Huh? Why?" I could feel my heart sink into my stomach. I was really looking forward to seeing him there every day.

"Because . . . you know. What happened back then. I . . . I can't believe your father let you and Delia audition," he said.

I stared hard at him. I'd never seen him like this before. Jake literally moonwalked through life. He never stressed over anything. But now he seemed genuinely frightened. "Jake, you mean—"

"That old house. Where they're filming. You don't want to be in that house, Claire. It isn't a joke. It's . . . dangerous."

He suddenly looked ten years old. His intense expression made me laugh.

"Seriously. Don't laugh. I think you should quit, too."

"Jake, we've been rehearsing in the house for a week. No dead people. No ghosts. It's all good."

"Three kids died in that house."

"Stop, Jake. Delia and I have been waiting for an opportunity like this forever. And we get to work with Lana deLurean and Jeremy Dane."

He shrugged. "Whatever floats your boat."

My fantasy night with Jake wasn't working out. He'd spoiled everything.

I turned and started to jog toward the pool house. "Later, Jake," I called to him. "Thanks for the advice. Glad you care so much."

I wanted to find Delia and go home. I searched for her around the pool, but she wasn't there. Did she wander down to the tennis courts with Shawn?

I turned back toward the house—and saw Jake with Annalee. She had a towel tied around her waist and was wringing out her wet hair. The two of them laughed about something. Then Annalee gave Jake a hug. She smoothed her wet hand down his cheek. He grinned back at her.

She was totally coming on to him.

And he was loving it.

I turned away and spotted Ross standing by himself by the pool house wall.

You ever just have an impulse? Maybe you're hurt or confused or angry and you have a sudden impulse to do something crazy?

"Hey, there you are," I said. I slid Ross's glass from his hand and took a long drink. I handed it back to him. Then I pushed him up against the wall, wrapped my hands around his neck, locked my lips on his, and started to kiss him.

Just an impulse. Really.

I turned and looked to see if Jake was watching. But he and Annalee had disappeared. So I pressed my mouth to Ross's and kissed him again.

I mean, why should the night be a *total* loss?

6

I SEE GHOSTS

"THERE ARE GHOSTS HERE," I said. "Can't you just feel them all around?"

And I knew as soon as I said it that Delia would roll her dark eyes and give me that look like, *Come on, Claire. Grow up.*

Delia gazed all around, pretending to be worried. "Ghosts? Should I be scared?"

We were wandering through the studio, searching for the wardrobe department, but lost as usual. Which made Delia laugh since my parents *run* the place. But that doesn't mean I have a map in my head. Sometimes I need a GPS to find the bathroom in the morning. I mean, we don't all have a brilliant sense of direction, do we?

We were both wearing the new Ray-Bans my dad was passing out to everyone on the set. Some kind of product placement thing. But the midday sun was so bright, I felt kind of dazed, and I kept bumping shoulders with Delia as we made our way through the crowded studio street.

Could I be any more excited about having an actual speaking part in *Mayhem Manor*? I don't think so. Like I said, this was my dream.

History lesson: I've had the acting bug since I was nine or ten. I've taken acting lessons and dance lessons and speech lessons, and I've been in every play production at school.

You'd think I'd get a little support from Mom and Dad since they're in the business. But they had a million reasons why I shouldn't be an actor. Maybe they were good reasons. I didn't care and I didn't listen.

I've begged and begged for a chance to audition. It took all these years, but I finally wore them down. They let me try out for *Mayhem Manor,* and I got the role of Darlene. Now I guess I have something to prove to them. Sure, it's only a low-budget horror film, but I'm going to rock the part.

Delia has the actress bug, too. Only a little different. She's had a bunch of modeling jobs. But she says her ambition is to be a tabloid star. I think that was a joke. She has a twisted sense of humor.

It's kind of a strange friendship. I think a lot of it is based on Delia rolling her eyes and laughing at me. She is very sarcastic, and I guess I'm the bubbly type. Or maybe it's that I get enthusiastic and she likes to stand aside and make comments.

We're more different than alike. I always say I'm Urban Outfitters and she's Juicy Couture. I don't even like to shop. If you want to know, Old Navy is fine for me.

I'm not exactly what you'd call drab or cute-challenged—but as I said, Delia is a total knockout. You can ask anyone to name the hottest girl at Beverly Hills Academy, and they'd have to be a total freak not to pick Delia.

She has short, perfect black hair with violet streaks on her bangs, huge black eyes, and beautiful red heart-shaped lips. And when the two of us go walking on Rodeo Drive, the tourists all stare at her and try to figure out which movie star she is.

Seriously. Last week a woman parked her Bentley in front of Armani and came hustling up to Delia. She stuck a piece of paper in front of her and asked for her autograph. And when Delia said, "I'm just a high school student," the woman laughed and pushed the paper in her face until she signed.

Delia and I passed the low, white stucco building with the green double doors. The commissary. A roar of voices poured out the open windows along with the smell of burgers and eggs on the fry grill.

"Why do you say there are ghosts here? I don't see any ghosts," Delia said, looking at me over the rims of her Ray-Bans. "I see the dog from that comedy they're shooting. Remember? We wandered onto the set by mistake?"

Ace, the black-and-white mutt, stood beside the commissary steps. Of course, he had a crowd around him. The dog gets crowds wherever he goes, and you can tell he loves it. He must be the most spoiled dog in Hollywood, which is saying a *lot*, right?

Four men wearing long red monk robes with hoods, all

talking at once, pushed past us as if they didn't see us and hurried into the commissary.

"I didn't mean *ghost* ghosts," I told Delia. "I meant the ghosts of all the stars who made films here. You know. Back in the day."

The studio was huge in the '30s and '40s. But it was pretty much abandoned, like a ghost town, after those three teenage actors were killed in 1960. My parents and Jake's parents took it over a few years after I was born. They named it WoodCast Studios. Get it? Combining our names— Woodlawn and Castellano.

"Can't you feel them?" I said. "All those beautiful people who worked here? I have such a magical feeling. How can you walk around a movie studio and not believe in magic?"

I knew I was risking another roll of her eyes, but I didn't care. "I mean, come on, Dee. Aren't we lucky working in a movie studio? The whole point of this place is to make magic happen."

"I thought the point was to find the costume department," Delia said.

"Hah." I gave her a shove and nearly knocked her off her stiletto heels.

I suddenly remembered when we bought those red shoes for her. One of our Saturday-afternoon shopping extravaganzas. We'd started out at some small boutiques in Westwood. But as usual when Delia was in a shopping mood (which is when she's awake), we ended up closer to home. First Jill Roberts on Beverly, then over to Barneys. And then, sure enough, there were these perfect shoes in Jimmy Choo's window. Delia spends a gazillion dollars on clothes, I think mainly because her mom is so thrifty and cheap.

"Magic everywhere, huh? I guess you're a lot more sensitive than me, Claire."

"You're just more cynical. I don't think it's babyish or crazy to be into magic."

We stopped to let a long shiny pink Cadillac convertible with enormous sharklike fins roll past. The dark-haired, suntanned driver flashed us a thumbs-up and a white, toothy grin as he passed.

"He's only a seven," Delia said. "Too slick."

Yes, we rate everyone we see. That's not so terrible, is it?

"When I was five, I had a birthday party at home," I said. "You weren't there, were you?"

She shook her head. The sunlight made her black hair gleam. "My parents didn't move to Beverly Hills till I was seven, remember?"

We turned the corner. Several white-shingled cottages lined the street. They were exec offices. I thought I saw the yellow-and-green costume building at the far end.

"We had this clown at the party," I continued. "I remember his huge red bow tie, and he had long floppy red shoes, like snorkeling flippers. And he did all these cool tricks with rings and coins and scarves. I mean, they were cool for five-year-olds. We'd probably think they were totally lame now."

"Probably," Delia murmured. She snickered. "Did he do balloon animals? I'm a freak for balloon animals."

"My whole kindergarten class was there," I said, ignoring her. "They loved the clown. He was a huge hit. And when he left, my parents called me to the door to say good-bye to him. I ran up to him and he leaned down. I remember his floppy bow tie hit me in the face. And he whispered something to me. He whispered, *Don't forget the magic.*"

Delia stopped walking. She pulled off her shades and squinted hard at me. "Why are you telling me this story? Am I supposed to feel warm and fuzzy or something?"

"It's just that I never forgot it," I said. "I was five, right? But all these years, I never forgot what he whispered in my ear. *Don't forget the magic.*"

Delia startled me by wrapping me in a hug. She let go quickly, grinning, and stepped back. "Claire, did you tell your shrink this story?"

"No," I said. "I—"

"Good. Because that would bore *him* to death, too!"

We both laughed. That's one reason I put up with a lot of crap from Delia. She makes me laugh.

My phone made a doorbell sound. I pulled it out and tilted the screen out of the sun. "A text from Shawn."

Delia made a gurgling sound.

I read the text: *"Want to hang out later?"*

"Huh? Shawn is texting *you*?"

I tucked the phone back into my bag. "Yeah. I didn't want to tell you. He keeps texting. I told him I'm not interested. Really, Dee. But he's such a jerk. He doesn't quit."

Delia uttered a cry. "He's texting *you*—not me? I

practically *jumped* him last night at Ross's party. Seriously. I don't get it. The more I come on to him, the more he comes on to *you*."

I pulled her into the shade of one of the cottages. "Dee, I've been waiting for you to spill. You know. About last night. The party. What happened with you and Shawn?"

She let out a groan. "Nothing happened."

"Nothing? That's why you didn't talk all the way home in the car?"

She shook her head. "It was . . . weird. I wasn't exactly like subtle. I mean, after we both had a few beers, I sat on his lap. Do you believe it? I *sat in his lap* in my bikini and put my hands around his neck."

I squinted at her. "And?"

"Well . . . we fooled around for a little while. And then he like lifted me off and stood up and said he had to go home and wax his board."

"Huh? What does that *mean*? Wax his board? Is that some kind of sex thing?"

"Shut up, stupid. He *really* wanted to go home and wax his surfboard. He got a new board yesterday. A triple wing-fish with a double concave bottom. He told me all about it. It has a rocker that's a lot like a shortboard."

My mouth was hanging open. "You shut up. You were sitting on his lap and he told you all this about his surfboard?"

She nodded.

"So what did *you* say?" I asked.

Delia shrugged. "What could I say? I said, 'Gnarly, dude.'

Then I went to find you to see how you were doing with Jake."

"We both struck out big-time." I sighed. "Everything is screwed up. You sit in Shawn's lap, and he keeps texting *me*. I try to tell Jake how I feel about him, and he only wants to ask me about *you*. What are we doing wrong?"

"Living," she replied.

That was more bitter than usual.

I studied her. She could have any guy at Beverly Hills Academy. Why was she so nuts over Shawn, a big hulk who only cared about waxing his board?

Delia sighed. We both sighed. It was a sighing festival.

I tried to think of something to take her mind off Shawn. But she was staring back to the end of the row of cottages.

I squeezed her arm. "What's wrong?"

"Speaking of ghosts," she whispered. "Look over there."

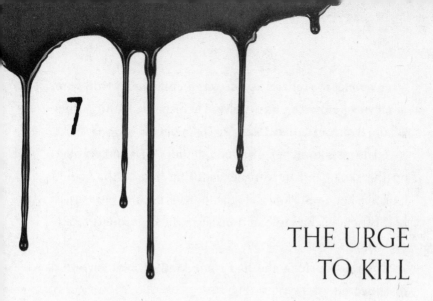

7

THE URGE
TO KILL

I SAW LANA DELUREAN WALKING toward us in a red mini-skirt and powder-blue camisole top. Her blond hair caught the sunlight. When she walked, her whole body wiggled, as if her bones somehow weren't connected.

Lana is one of the stars of *Mayhem Manor*, and she's beautiful in a pale, anorexic, arms-like-broom-handles kind of way. She's got to be at least thirty, but she still plays teen roles. She has a sexy, whispery voice, which she must practice at home, big blue eyes that are probably helped by contacts, and the cheekbones of a runway model.

As she approached, I noticed how tiny she was, much smaller than she appears on screen. *She's a mini-person,* I thought, *with a maxi-ego.*

Maybe I wasn't being fair.

Lana has had some rough times. I Googled her right

after we met for rehearsal. She was a child star. Made a ton of movies before she was twelve. Then she had a hit Disney Channel sitcom called *That's My Girlfriend* for two years.

Little girls loved her. They bought her DVDs and grabbed up the skirts and tops in her clothing line so they could look like her. Even Lana Cologne for Kids became *humongous*. Lots of schools had to ban it because the classrooms totally reeked of it.

Then at fourteen she had some kind of meltdown and disappeared.

I checked IMDb and Wikipedia as well as Google, but no one had the details. She disappeared from TV and movies and department stores, and of course, kids forgot about her practically overnight.

Now, here was Lana deLurean starring in a low-budget horror film for my parents. I guess it was her comeback project, but she sure didn't seem happy about it. Lana still acted like she was on the cover of *People* and *Us* every week, like she was the Tween Queen of Hollywood or Burbank or whatever.

"Who's that guy with her?" I whispered to Delia.

A tanned young man, bald as a lightbulb, wearing all white—white suit, white shirt, white shoes—trailed closely behind Lana.

"Haven't you seen him before?" Delia whispered back. "That's Pablo. Her psychic. She brings him everywhere."

I didn't have time to reply. Lana stepped up, peering at us through her red heart-shaped shades. "How's it going?" she breathed.

What was that powerful lemony scent? Could she possibly be wearing Lana Cologne for Kids?

"Good," Delia and I said in unison.

Pablo stood close behind Lana, as if making shade for her. He had a sparkly diamond stud in his right nostril. His intense dark eyes moved from Delia to me, as if he was studying us, reading our minds.

"I'm sorry. Remind me of your names," Lana said.

The scent was so strong, it burned my nose. I told her our names—for at least the tenth time. We'd been rehearsing together for a week.

"Oh, right." She smiled at me. Her teeth were bright white, shiny as a car. "Your father is Sy Woodlawn."

"And my mom is Rita." *Why did I say that?*

Lana scratched her skinny arm with perfect long, red fingernails. "It was so neat of your dad to give both of you parts in the picture."

I felt a stab of anger in my chest. "He didn't give us parts," I snapped. "We auditioned for them. Les Bachman gave us the parts." Les is the director.

She squinted at me like I was speaking a foreign language. Behind her, Pablo picked at his teeth with a finger. A fly landed on his shoulder, ruining the perfect whiteness of his being.

"Are we late for rehearsal?" Lana asked. "I think lunch is over."

"Simon Ferris, the wardrobe guy, sent us to pick up our costumes," I said. "But we got turned around."

Lana laughed. She had a surprising laugh, like a horse

whinny. "Your parents run the studio, and you don't know where the wardrobe department is?"

Pablo chuckled, too. Like Lana had made a great joke.

"I have the *worst* sense of direction," I confessed. "I get lost in my own bedroom closet."

That was supposed to be a joke, but only Delia laughed. And it was an obvious fake laugh.

I don't know why Lana made me feel so uncomfortable. Well...actually, I *do* know why. It was because she could never say anything honest or be real for one second. Everything she said was an act, like she was posing in front of a camera. Why couldn't she just relax and be a human?

"It's so cold in the old mansion," she said. "I start to shiver as soon as I get on the set. I'll bet the camera can see my goose bumps." She hugged herself and made her whole body shiver.

"Claire thinks it stays cold in there because of the ghosts," Delia said. "You know. The ghosts of the three actors who were killed."

That got Pablo's attention. He gazed intently at me. "Ghosts? Do you believe in ghosts?"

I nodded. "Yeah. Kind of."

That made Lana shiver again. "I don't like filming in a haunted house. But I guess it will get press. All the reporters will think it's a great angle. We'll be on *Access Hollywood* and everything. And everyone will be talking about how we made a horror film in a place where true horror took place."

Whoa.

That was the longest speech I ever heard Lana deLurean give. "Do *you* really think the mansion is haunted?" I asked her.

Her red lips formed a small O. She stared hard at me. "I . . . don't know." She turned to Pablo. As if he had the answer.

"There are ghosts all around this old studio," he said, gesturing. "I can feel them. I hear them whispering to me."

"Hey, that's just what Claire said!" Delia exclaimed. "Maybe Claire is psychic, too."

"I'm not really psychic," Pablo said, rubbing his bald head like he was polishing it. "I can just feel things that others miss. Like vibrations. Messages in the air."

Lana's expression turned hard again. I could see her jaw muscles clench. I guessed she didn't like it when the conversation wasn't about her. Or maybe she didn't like to share Pablo.

"We'd better go," she said. "You know how Les gets when I'm not on the set on time. He has palpitations. Really."

Les has palpitations when you say good morning to him. He's totally wired all the time. People are always telling him to try decaf.

Lana turned to me. "I hope you find the costume building. Don't get lost." A tight smile crossed her face. "We need you extras. You're more important than you think."

Extras? Delia and I have speaking roles.

We watched Lana wriggle off. Pablo glanced back at us, then hurried to keep up with her.

Delia bumped up against me. "Do we hate her?" she said. "Should we kill her?"

"*Being* her is punishment enough," I said.

And then a voice behind us startled me. "Who do you want to kill? Can I help?"

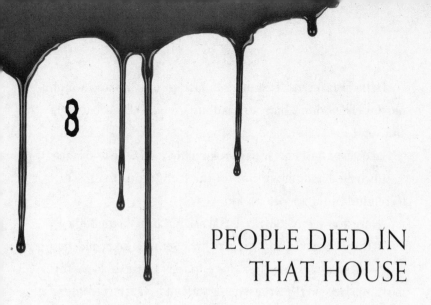

8

PEOPLE DIED IN
THAT HOUSE

DELIA AND I BOTH CRIED OUT. I spun around and saw Jake grinning at us.

"Jake? You're here?" Delia said. Then she remembered. "Oh, right. You're working on the film, too."

I could see the hurt expression on his face. Like *How could Delia forget about me?*

"Actually, I'm interning with Zack Fox," Jake said.

Zack Fox is the film editor for *Mayhem Manor*. And he's my dad's best friend. Dad arranged for Jake to work with Zack this summer.

"Zack is like all over the new editing software," Jake said. "He's going to teach me everything."

"You want to be a film editor?" Delia asked.

"For sure. I want to learn *everything*. Hey, you know I'm going to be a film major. My parents already got me some interviews at USC."

Delia snickered. "Film majors just go to class and watch movies. They don't have to read any books." That made me snicker, too.

Jake's eyes flashed. "You're looking hot today," he told Delia.

I brushed a clump of lint off the front of his t-shirt. Just to remind him I was there, too.

"Have you seen Shawn?" Delia asked. "Is he home today?"

"I think he's visiting his dad in Laguna," Jake told her. "He went down there after Ross's party. He texted me this morning. He said the waves were good but it was too crowded."

Laguna surfers are in their wet suits and in the water before the sun comes up. They're all total fanatics. Shawn is a fanatic, but he also likes his sleep.

"Is he coming home tonight?" Delia asked.

Jake shrugged. "Beats me. Why are you always asking me about Shawn? How come you don't ask how *I'm* doing?"

"How are you doing?" I chimed in, trying to get into the conversation. But Jake only had eyes for Delia.

"I'm kind of worried about Shawn," she said, frowning. "I think he's still stressing about his parents splitting up. You know. And his dad moving down to Laguna."

"Yeah, it's been tough on him," Jake said.

I knew Delia wasn't really that worried. She was just seriously hot for Shawn.

I tugged Jake's arm. "Dee and I are going to be late for rehearsal. Point us to the wardrobe building. We're supposed to be on the set."

Jake's expression changed. "You shouldn't go in that old

house," he said. "Seriously. We're all insane to go in there. I told you last night at the party. Mayhem Manor is totally cursed."

Delia rolled her eyes. "You and Claire should be a couple. You could compare ghost stories."

Hint, hint. Yes. WE should be a couple.

"I usually don't believe in that stuff. But there's got to be three dead people haunting that place," Jake said.

"Stop it, Jake. Not funny," I said.

"Who's joking? Three people our age died in that house. Do you really think they were all killed by *accidents*? They're waiting in there. Waiting to avenge their deaths."

Jake looked so serious, I had to laugh. "Jake, you sound like a really lame horror movie."

"Seriously? Seriously? You're laughing about it?" he said.

I gave him a hard shove. "Lighten up, dude."

History lesson number two: After the deaths of the three young actors, the film was stopped immediately. And the old mansion was never used again. Not even for exterior shots. No one wanted to go near it. People said it was cursed.

The house just sat in the shadows at the back of the studio, rotting and falling apart. For some reason, it was never torn down. Maybe people were too superstitious to wreck it.

It was my dad who had the idea to do a remake of *Mayhem Manor*. To make the film again inside the original mansion.

"Think of the publicity," my parents said. "Remaking a movie in the same house where people were actually killed. What a total winner."

They talked about it nonstop. Breakfast. Dinner. I mean, they were talking like they had the biggest blockbuster.

When I told them the whole idea creeped me out, they said it creeped them out, too. That's why it was a good idea.

Now, standing outside the row of exec cottages, I squinted at Jake through my sunglasses. He was so adorable. I just wanted a chance to let him know how I felt. "Jake," I said, "how are you getting home tonight? You driving home with your parents? Can I have a ride?"

Jake and I live next door to each other on Coldwater Canyon Drive. I told you our families are close. Our parents work together, and they live side by side. It's no wonder Jake only thinks of me as a sister.

"No, I'm not going home. Zack is taking me to see his editing studio at his house."

I didn't give up. "When are you getting back? Do you want to maybe hang later?"

He scratched his head. "I don't think so. I'm getting back pretty late."

He had his eye on Delia. She was smoothing lip gloss on her lips. She wasn't paying any attention to Jake at all.

"Later," Jake said. "The wardrobe building is right up there." He pointed. Then he turned and started toward Mayhem Manor.

"Hey, Jake?" He stopped and turned back when I called him. "Do you really think those three kids are haunting Mayhem Manor, waiting for revenge?"

He narrowed his eyes at me. "We'll soon see, won't we?"

9

WEARING A DEAD GIRL'S CLOTHES

"HE NEVER TOOK HIS EYES OFF YOU," I told Delia. "Jake never looked at me. I don't think he even knew I was there."

Delia shrugged. "I didn't notice. You sure?"

"Yeah. I'm sure. He stared at you like ... like he was hungry."

Delia laughed. "Hungry? You're getting weird."

"I've seen him stare at a pizza with the same longing expression. Really."

"Claire, you think Jake is a *cannibal*?"

"It's not a joke," I snapped. "I'm really kind of nutty about him. I mean, I get all fluttery, like in a bad chick-lit novel. But he doesn't even *look* at me. Look. Is my face red? I can feel myself blushing when I see him. That's sick, right?"

Delia's dark eyes met mine. "Listen, Claire, if you're really into him, you have to let him know it."

"What do you think I was doing? I tried last night at the party. And just now. You saw me. I asked for a ride. I asked if he wanted to hang out later. I've been trying to get him alone for weeks, Dee."

"Well, get him drunk and attack him."

It was my turn to roll my eyes. "You're such a big help. *Not.*"

How could we not see the wardrobe building? For one thing, it was two stories tall and bright green-and-yellow stucco. And it had a huge sign over the double front doors that said WARDROBE DEPARTMENT.

Delia pulled open the door, and I followed her inside. We stepped into a wide, brightly lit room with endless racks of clothing and costumes of all colors and types.

My eyes stopped on a row of old-fashioned frilly white bonnets on hooks along one wall. A gorilla costume had been tossed over a rack of black leather bomber jackets. The next rack held shimmery green-and-gold party dresses. A mountain of dark pants was piled on the floor near the far wall.

I took a few steps along the front of the room, my eyes moving over the long costume racks. "Is anybody here?" I called. My voice sounded hollow in the big room.

The film is set in the '60s. We're supposed to look like '60s teenagers. But what did they look like? How could we ever find the right clothes in this incredible jumble?

"Hey, anybody?" Delia called. "Anybody here?"

A woman came hurrying out from a row of colorful party dresses. She was short and had a pile of henna-red hair, round brown eyes, a nose that seemed too long for her face, and a friendly smile. She was wrapping a silky orange scarf around her shoulders that clashed badly with her hair. She wore a loose-fitting brown skirt over black tights. I guessed she was in her forties or maybe fifties.

"Can I help you, young lady?" She had a very young voice, tiny and bright. "Are you in *Please Don't?*"

I shook my head. "No. Hi. I'm Claire Woodlawn."

She fiddled with the big scarf. "Oh, my goodness gracious. Of course. Claire. I'm Betty Hecht. I was at your fifth birthday party. At your house. Your old house. The one in the Valley. I don't think I've seen you since then. You've grown a bit."

I laughed. "I guess."

"I heard you're in *Mayhem Manor*," she said. "And you're Delia, right?"

Delia nodded. "Nice to meet you."

"I have your clothes ready," Betty said. "Simon Ferris ordered them yesterday. Now we have to get them fitted." She turned and headed to a shelf against the wall. Then she turned back. "Are you two afraid to go in there? Afraid to go in that old house?"

I shook my head. "This is my dream," I said. "To be a film actor. It's what I've always wanted. My parents finally said I could try. So . . . I'm not going to be afraid."

Delia squinted at Betty. "Do you think we *should* be afraid?"

Betty didn't answer. She pulled two wrapped packages

off the shelf. "Which one of you plays Geena and which is Darlene?"

"I'm Darlene," I said. "The one who always acts tough."

"It's typecasting," Delia joked.

Betty handed us each a package. She pointed. "You'll find dressing rooms back there. Put them on and we'll see what needs to be done to make them fit."

Delia and I walked to the back of the room and stepped into side-by-side dressing rooms. I pulled the curtain shut behind me. The room was just a closet with a wood bench on one side and a full-length mirror on the other.

I opened the package and tugged out a long straight skirt, charcoal gray and pleated at the bottom, and a bright pink top, lacy around the collar.

"Let me check them out when you're dressed," Betty called.

I pulled on the skirt, then the top. The skirt was a little snug at the waist and came down just below my knees. Weird length. The top was loose-fitting and not sexy at all.

I turned to gaze at myself in the mirror—but something was wrong.

My eyes refused to focus. I gazed at myself through a thick mist. At first, I thought it was the mirror. I rubbed it with the sleeve of my top.

But the fog didn't clear. And I suddenly began to feel very weird, as if I were floating in the mist. Not really floating off the floor but hovering far away from the mirror... far away from my reflection.

I heard a whisper of sound, like when you hold a seashell to your ear. Just a sudden rush of wind in my ears as I floated farther from the mirror.

And then Betty's voice broke through the dressing-room curtain at my back. "Hey, girls—you know those are costumes from the original movie?"

It took a while for her words to come through the fog. I realized my brain was fogged like my vision.

Did one of the murdered girls wear this skirt? This top?

Am I dressed in a dead girl's costume?

"Betty?" I tried to call to her.

But the rush of sound in my ears rose like a wave crashing against the shore. A constant roar I couldn't shut out.

And over the roar, I thought I heard a whispered voice. A girl's voice, very distant and frightened. A tiny voice over the rush of wind. Coming from the clothing? No. That's impossible.

What was she saying? I could barely hear her . . .

"Go away. Go awaaaaay . . ."

10

"WHAT DID YOU DO TO ME?"

I MUST HAVE SCREAMED. I didn't hear myself.

Betty Hecht tore open the curtain. "Are you okay?"

The rushing in my ears stopped. The fog vanished. I blinked at myself in the mirror. My whole body was shaking.

"Yeah. I'm all right. I guess I freaked a little about wearing these clothes. You know. From a dead girl."

She snickered. "Well, she was alive when she wore them. Step out and let me see you."

I took a deep breath to steady myself. *Claire, you imagined that voice.*

Then I walked out of the dressing room, adjusting the top. I brushed Delia's dressing-room curtain. "Dee, everything okay?"

She pulled back the curtain. She hadn't changed yet. She sat on the bench with her phone to her ear. "I have to take this call. It's my modeling agent." She waved me away. "Go on without me. I'll catch up." She pulled the curtain shut.

"You look perfect," Betty said to me. She tugged at the top of my skirt. "A little snug. Can you breathe?"

"Sure. No problem," I said.

"Follow me. I'll sign you out," Betty said, starting to the counter in front. "Simon wants you to go to makeup next. Do you know where the trailer is?"

"I . . . think so," I replied.

I thanked her, and she said it was so nice to see me. "I hope the movie goes well," she said. I could tell by the way she gazed into my eyes that she was worried about the whole thing.

Maybe she believed Mayhem Manor was cursed or something. Or maybe she was just a worrier.

I didn't have time to think about it. I stepped into the bright sunlight and started to walk around the side of the building. I shielded my eyes with one hand. I realized I'd left my Ray-Bans in the dressing room. I decided to come back for them later.

A small white trailer stood in the shadow of the wardrobe building. I blinked at it. It had no sign, no markings on it at all.

Strange, I thought. *Les told me the makeup trailer was at the side of Mayhem Manor.*

I decided they must have moved it. I let out a long breath. The old skirt was tighter than I'd thought. Maybe it would encourage me to lose some weight.

I climbed the three metal steps to the trailer door, then hesitated. Should I knock? I decided to go right in.

I pulled open the door and leaned inside. It took a few seconds for my eyes to adjust after the bright sunlight. Inside the trailer, I saw a wall of shelves filled with bottles and jars, all different colors.

Yes. This must be the right place, I decided. I stepped through the doorway and pulled the door closed behind me. I turned—and saw the creature sitting behind a low desk.

I gasped.

It took me a few seconds to realize it wasn't a creature. It was a very hairy little man. I felt my face grow hot. I was embarrassed that I had uttered a gasp.

But he was a strange-looking little dude. He had to be no more than five feet tall, and he was covered in hair. I mean, he had like a black shrub falling over his head, poking out in all directions. And a stubbly black beard on his round face. And his sleeveless blue wifebeater shirt showed off hairy black arms and a lot of black chest fur.

OMG. Anybody could have mistaken him for a bear or something. Trust me. He was a real hairy bowling ball.

I backed against the door. In case the beast attacked.

But when he spoke, he had a soft, high voice, and he smiled, and I could see he was human, after all. Or at least *almost* human.

"Welcome, welcome," he said. "What can I do for you today?"

He had tiny hands with curly hair on the backs, and he plucked at the front of his tight shirt as he gazed up at me.

"Simon Ferris sent me," I said. And then I stopped. And squinted at him. "Have I seen you somewhere before?"

He scratched his beard. "I don't think so."

"Haven't we met?" I had the strongest feeling.

"No," he said. "Who are you?"

I studied his face. He had dark eyes under heavy black eyebrows and a flat nose. His mouth was lost somewhere in his beard.

"From *Mayhem Manor*," I said. "I'm Claire Woodlawn. I'm playing Darlene."

He murmured something under his breath. It sounded like, "Darlene was a nice girl." But I knew I hadn't heard right.

"I'm Benny Puckerman. Everyone calls me Puck." He nodded his head as if taking a short bow.

My eyes darted over the shelves all around him, the small bottles and jars. Hundreds of them. I realized none of the jars or bottles had labels.

"What is all this?" I asked. "Is this makeup? This is the makeup trailer, right?"

He snickered. He scratched his beard. "No, I don't have any makeup here."

"I-I'm in the wrong trailer?" I stammered. I wished he would stop staring. He didn't blink. The hairy little guy was giving me the creeps. "Well, what is in all these bottles?"

"It's my potions," he said. He stood up. He kept his eyes on mine. "Do you believe in potions, Claire?"

"No. No way. I mean . . . well . . . I don't know. I mean . . ." I tried to back up but there was no room. I bumped a shelf of bottles behind me.

"Well, I do," he said. "I believe in them because I know they work." He snickered again. Not a pleasant sound. He picked up a small blue bottle and rolled it in his pudgy hand. "They work. They work."

I wanted to get out of there. He took another step toward me. I wondered if Delia was coming soon. "Wh-what kind of potions?" I stammered.

A smile spread under his black beard. "All kinds."

He set down the blue bottle and picked up a tiny jar next to it. He raised it to my face. It had a glittery gray powder inside. He shook it in front of me.

"It's a love potion," he said. "You interested? Maybe try it on someone?"

I couldn't hold back my laugh. This dude was insane. "A love potion? For real?"

He nodded. The strange grin appeared frozen on his face. "It works. It really works." He held it close and gazed at the gray powder.

"You pour it on someone, see. It only takes a little bit. You spill a few flakes on them. Then they will fall in love— *madly* in love—with the first person they see."

I laughed again. Nervous laughter. Was he *kidding* me?

"That's Shakespeare," I said. "Nice try, Mr. Puckerman. But we read that play in tenth grade. The fairy puts the love potion on the girl's eyes so she'll fall in love with the guy who's crazy about her. But when she wakes up, the first thing she sees is a guy who's been turned into a donkey. And she falls madly in love with the donkey. We read it last year."

Puckerman shook his head. "That's just a play. This is real."

I gazed at the jar in his hand. "What is it *really*?"

He frowned. "I don't make up stories. And I don't lie." He waved a hand, motioning to the shelves. "These potions are the real thing. Let me demonstrate."

He moved quickly. Before I could duck out of the way, he dove toward me, raised a furry paw above my head, tilted a small bottle, and shook powdery silver flakes onto my shoulders.

"N-nooo," I stammered in total panic. "What did you *do*? What is that?"

"It's the love potion," he answered.

I felt a tingling in my shoulders, like a mild electrical shock. My skin prickled as the feeling ran down my whole body. The bottles and jars became a blur of color all around me.

"What did you do to me?" I cried, my voice muffled, distant. "What did you *do* to me?"

11

HOUSE OF DEATH

I GAZED DOWN AT THE LITTLE MAN, at his adorable black beard, at the awesome wild tuft of hair on his head, at his beautiful face with its softly glowing dark eyes and gleaming smile.

A strong emotion swept over me. I wanted to grab him in my arms and pull him close, wrap him in a tight hug and tell him how wonderful he was.

"Claire, you and I have things to do later," he said in that sweet, sweet voice. "Not yet. Not yet. But soon."

I'd never felt this way about anyone. My heart was pounding. My hands were clammy. I couldn't resist him.

I squeezed my hands over his thick shoulders. He had beautiful spiky back hair poking out from his t-shirt. "Can I . . . Can I . . ." I worked up my courage. "Can I kiss you? Can I hold you?"

He slid out of my grasp. "I'm just demonstrating the potion to you. Next time, you won't question my power."

"Please—" I begged, my voice trembling with feeling. "I just want to hold you close to me. I want to kiss you. I want to feel your beard against my face. Please—"

He raised his arm and sprinkled another powder, this time on my hair. The room blurred again. I felt my throat tighten. My stomach gurgled and growled.

Puckerman slowly came back into focus. He had beads of sweat on his ugly beard. His eyes were wet like oysters. He scratched his greasy hair. Gross.

"Get away from me," I snapped. "What did you just do?"

"I'll be calling you soon," he said. "Believe me, you won't enjoy it."

"Explain it to me—"

"You have to face your fate, Claire. You *do* believe in fate, don't you? Mayhem Manor is a house of death. When you enter a house of death, you must expect to die."

"You—you're crazy!" I cried. "You're *sick*. I'll call security. Really. I'll call the studio guards."

His dark eyes burned into mine, like he was trying to hypnotize me. "No, you won't," he said softly. "You won't call security."

Again, his hand flew over my head. This time, a black powder rained onto my hair. Again, my head tingled and itched.

I tried to twist away. But there was no room. I was totally trapped.

"That's a *forgetting* potion," Puckerman said. He spun the

cap back over the little bottle. He flashed me a toothy smile. "You'll forget this happened, Claire."

I stared at him, my mouth hanging open, my whole body shaking. I couldn't move. I couldn't breathe.

The room suddenly went out of focus. Like a bad photograph. I squinted hard, struggling to make it clear again.

No, I thought. *No way. I won't forget. I won't forget.* I gritted my teeth so hard my jaw hurt. I struggled against the potion.

"You've forgotten already, haven't you," Puckerman said.

I pretended to be confused. "Forgot about what?" I said. It was a lie. I remembered everything.

Without warning, he pushed open the trailer door and gave me a gentle shove outside. I stumbled down the stairs and before I could regain my balance, bumped into Delia.

"Is this the makeup trailer?" she asked. "Why do you look so weird?"

"I don't know," I said. "I . . . I mean, no. It's not. Wrong trailer." I wanted to think about the whole thing before I told Delia about it.

She blocked my path. She wore a man's starched white dress shirt over straight-legged jeans. Her costume. She grabbed for my hand. "What is that, Claire? What have you got?"

She pulled a slender gray pill bottle from my hand. She studied the unmarked bottle. "Did you get this inside that trailer?"

"Yes. I stole it." I grabbed the bottle from her and spun it in my hand. "It's a potion. I took it off a shelf in there."

Delia rolled her eyes. "I should have known. Another one of your crazy—"

"No," I said. "It's real, Dee. I took it from the little guy in there. He tried to make me forget. But I concentrated. I fought off his spell. My mind is foggy, but . . . I—I took a love potion."

She burst out laughing. "Give me some. I'll try it on Shawn."

I felt a surge of excitement in my chest. "And I'll pour some on Jake," I said. "No joke. We'll get them together, and we'll try it. We'll try the potion on them."

"Why not?" Delia said. "What do we have to lose?"

12

THEY TRY THE LOVE POTION

THE NEXT DAY, WE HAD A FREE DAY. The set was closed for tech rehearsal. Les Bachman was preparing for the first day of shooting.

I slept till noon. I would have slept later, but the two pool service guys were having some sort of argument outside my window. Something about chlorine tabs.

I pulled on a pair of white short shorts and a sleeveless yellow tee. Then I rounded up Delia, Jake, and Shawn, and I drove us all to Malibu. The four of us squeezed into a booth at Ruby's Shake Shack on the pier.

What a day. The sun over the ocean. Chocolate milk shakes all around and maybe the best cheeseburgers in L.A.

Shawn was desperate to get to the beach. "My wet suit's in the back of your car," he said, wiping hamburger juice off his chin. "But I know a shack five minutes from here where they'll rent you guys stuff."

"Rent us what?" I said. "Shawn, did you notice we're not wearing swimsuits?"

Shawn snickered. "We could find an empty beach. You won't *need* bathing suits."

"Shut up," Delia said, but she grinned at him.

Shawn stared out at the white-capped waves. Jake tried to start a cheeseburger discussion: Whose is better—Ruby's, The Apple Pan, or In-N-Out Burger?

"Jake," I said, "we have the same discussion every time we come here."

He grinned at me. "So?"

I tried to squeeze his hand over the table. But he picked up his cheeseburger with it. He had his eyes on Delia.

I felt totally tense. My lunch was sitting in my throat. I reached into my bag and wrapped my fingers around the little potion bottle.

Was I really going to do this?

I tried to signal to Delia with my eyes. But she was watching Shawn.

Suddenly, Jake stared at me, and his expression turned serious. "Listen, I found some papers on my mom's desk," he said in a voice just above a whisper. "I wasn't supposed to see them. My parents never want to tell me anything serious."

I squinted at him. "Papers? Like what kind of papers?"

"All sorts of financial stuff. It said the studio is going bankrupt."

My mouth dropped open. "Shut up."

"You're joking," Delia said.

Jake shook his head. "*Mayhem Manor* has to be a smash hit. Or our parents will go out of business."

I could feel my face grow hot. "Oh, wow. I didn't realize it was that bad."

"It's scary," Jake said. "The papers said our parents have their *own* money invested in this thing. That means if the film goes into the toilet . . ."

Delia finished the sentence for him. "They might have to sell your houses? You might have to move away?"

I patted her on the shoulder. "That's Delia," I said. "Always looking on the bright side."

"Are you going to finish that?" Shawn asked Delia, jabbing a finger at her plate. He obviously hadn't been listening to a word we said. He didn't wait for her to answer. He took the cheeseburger from her hands and tilted it to his face.

Jake's phone bleeped. He pulled it from his pocket. "Hey, it's a text from Annalee Franklin." He read it out loud: "*Where r u?*"

I felt the blood pulse at my temples. Every time I thought of Annalee, I pictured her showing off her bod, swimming almost naked in Ross Harper's pool.

And now she was after Jake. I'd made the mistake of telling her that I was crushing on him. Annalee was such a jealous person. She always wanted everything I wanted.

She was always stealing boyfriends. And now she wanted Jake, who wasn't even my boyfriend.

I'd known Annalee since kindergarten. I tried to like her. I really did. But she wasn't a nice person. And now I watched Jake texting her back, and I wondered if the two of them had already hooked up.

Time for the love potion. Definitely.

I gripped the bottle and pulled it from my bag. I held it over my lap beneath the table. My heart started to flutter in my chest. As if I'd swallowed a hummingbird.

I leaned over to Delia, beside me in the booth, and whispered in her ear. "Potion time."

We had concocted a plan. A genius plan.

Under the table, I twisted the cap off the potion bottle and dropped it into my lap. Then I quickly raised the bottle to the tabletop.

"Jake, look at me," I said.

He crinkled his eyes. "Huh?"

"Look at me and don't turn away," I said.

I didn't give him a chance to ask any questions. I dipped two fingers into the bottle, lifted out a few flakes—and dropped them onto the top of his head.

"Hey—what's up with that?" he cried, eyes on the bottle in my hand.

I didn't answer. I slipped the potion to Delia. She dipped her fingers into the bottle.

"Shawn, can you take your eyes off Claire for a minute?" she asked in a sexy whisper.

Shawn had been staring at me, but now he obediently turned, and Delia sprinkled a few flakes onto the front of his blond hair.

He laughed. "Was that pepper? Why'd you do that?"

"Just keep looking at me," Delia instructed. She reached across the table, grabbed the sides of his face, and held him in place.

"Claire, is this some kind of joke?" Jake said. "I don't get it."

"You will," I said, tucking the bottle into my bag.

Then Delia and I just sat there, staring at each boy, waiting . . . waiting for the love.

13

"CAN I HIT YOU?"

NO ONE SAID A WORD. We just stared at one another across the table.

I couldn't take the suspense. I felt about to burst. I broke the silence. "Jake? Do you feel strange or anything?" My voice shook.

"Who wants to know?" he snapped.

My throat felt dry. That wasn't the response I expected.

Shawn scowled at Delia. "What are *you* looking at, fat face?"

Delia uttered a cry. "Huh? 'Fat face'?"

I shook my head, trying to force away my confusion. "Jake, I've been thinking about you a lot," I said.

"Shut up, jerk," he replied. "Shut your ugly pie hole."

"Wh-why are you saying those things?" I cried.

He stuck his face close to mine. "Because you're dumb?"

Shawn laughed. "They're both idiots." He and Jake bumped

knuckles. "Can we go get boards and ride some waves now? Why are we wasting our time with these losers?"

Delia flashed me a worried glance. Then she turned back to Shawn. She took his hand. She didn't want to give up. "You know, I kind of have a thing about you."

Shawn grabbed a French fry off his plate and shoved it into her nose.

Delia uttered a choked gasp and jerked back against the booth.

"Hey, now you're starting to look good!" Shawn said.

Both boys hee-hawed.

"Stop it! Stop it!" I cried.

"Just shut up and go away," Jake said. "Take a hike. Give us a break. Why not take a jump off the pier?"

"They both make me want to blow my lunch," Shawn said.

Delia whipped around angrily and grabbed me by the shoulders. "What have you done?" she screamed. "Claire, what have you done?"

My heart was thudding so hard, I couldn't breathe. "The potion—" I said. "Did I steal the wrong one? Did I—?"

I turned to see Jake on his feet, leaning over the table, waving his fist at me. "Can I hit you just once?" he said, in a low growl I'd never heard from him before. "Please? Can I hit you just once? I'll fix your ugly nose for you."

I could see he was serious. Delia and I were trapped in the booth. We couldn't escape.

"Jake, please—" I said. "Sit down. Please. Do you remember who I am? Remember? I'm your friend?"

He shook the fist. He had a hideous hard expression tightening his features. "Just once. I just need to hit you once."

"No—Jake. Don't!" I raised both hands to protect myself.

But with a furious cry, he pulled his arm back—and swung his fist at my face.

14

AN EVIL PRESENCE

"NOOOOO!"

I ducked away.

The fist sailed over my shoulder and hit the back of the booth.

I kept my arms raised, shielding my face.

Jake stood across the table, eyes on me, breathing hard.

Was he going to swing at me again?

No. His expression softened. He let out a long sigh, like air escaping a tire. He blinked a few times. Then he sank back onto his seat.

Shawn rubbed his cheeks. He scratched his head. "What just happened?" he asked Delia and me.

Jake stared at me, his eyes kind of blank. Like he was dazed. "Whoa," he murmured. "Whoa."

"Why are you two staring at us like that?" Shawn asked. "Do I have lettuce stuck to my teeth or something?" He rubbed his teeth.

"Did we pay for lunch?" Jake asked.

Delia and I exchanged glances. The potion's spell had worn off. Thank goodness we'd used only a few flakes.

What had I done? Stolen the wrong potion. This was the opposite of a love potion. Was it a *hate* potion?

"Let's roll. Let's pay the check," Jake said.

"Are you feeling okay?" I asked.

He nodded. "Sure. Let's pay the check."

"You're suddenly in a hurry?"

"Yeah. I'm meeting up with Annalee."

We all chipped in and paid for lunch. Then we made our way out of the restaurant. As we walked to my car, I hung back with Delia. "Well, *that* went well," I said.

The first day of shooting. Were Delia and I excited? Does a butter fly?

I drove to Burbank, parked the car in the studio lot, and we started to jog toward Mayhem Manor. At the end of the path, I could see the twin gray towers rising up in the distance. Like giant bat wings. The old mansion stayed dark, even in the brightest sunshine.

A cart rolled by with a large movie projector strapped to the back. And I saw Jake's dad, in a dark business suit as always, walking with two other business-type dudes, waving a sheet of paper in their faces and talking rapidly as they walked toward his cottage office. I waved but he didn't see me.

A few minutes later, the gray mansion and its tall towers loomed over us, and we stepped into its shadow. The air instantly grew colder, and the stale smell of mold and mildew of the rotting shingles on the front wall invaded my nose.

"I'm a little wired," I said. "I mean, I dreamed about this day, but now I'm really scared. You dreamed about it, too, right?"

"No," Delia said. "I always wanted to be a princess."

"Funny."

"Who's joking?"

I gasped as someone stepped out of the shadows. It took me a few seconds to recognize Pablo, Lana deLurean's psychic. Again, he was dressed in a silky white suit, but he had pulled a blue-and-white Dodgers cap over his bald head.

"Hello," he said. "I didn't mean to startle you."

I pulled off my sunglasses. "Dark here," I murmured. "Hard to see."

Delia eyed him suspiciously. "Aren't you going inside?"

He shut his eyes. "I feel bad things about this house. I can feel the presence of something very evil." He opened his eyes. "Do you feel it, too?"

"Not really," I said.

"Lana went inside?" Delia asked.

He nodded with a sigh. "She wouldn't listen to me. I warned her this wasn't the right day to go in there. But she said the movie came first. She was angry with me. But . . ." His voice trailed off.

"We have to go in, too," I said.

Delia scowled at him. "Why do you want to scare people?"

He blinked. "I have a responsibility. I have to speak what I feel, what I sense. I must be honest."

He spread his hand over Delia's forehead. "Shut your eyes," he said. "Listen hard. Concentrate. Do you feel anything?"

"Yes, I feel your hand on my forehead."

He didn't laugh. He removed his hand. "The evil here at this house is so strong," he said, gazing from Delia to me.

Over his shoulder, I saw the sign on the front door of the mansion: LIVE SET. DO NOT ENTER IF RED LIGHT IS ON. A red lightbulb had been installed at the top of the wooden door. It wasn't lit.

"Pablo, it's just a house," I said. "Just a neglected, old house."

"And now it's just a movie set," Delia added.

His eyes flared. "No, it isn't," he snapped. "It's a graveyard, ladies. It's a living graveyard."

And with those words, Delia and I pulled open the front door and stepped inside.

15

"WE'LL SLICE HER IN HALF"

BACK IN 1960, MAYHEM MANOR was built on the back of the studio lot on a wide, empty field that wasn't being used. It was meant to be a movie set, but the carpenters built an entire house with solid walls and floors and stairways that led to a basement and a second-floor attic.

It was designed to look like the scariest haunted house ever built. The ceilings are cracked, and giant spiders and tarantulas hang down on long strings from a tangle of silvery cobwebs. The stairways are narrow and winding, and the steps are steep. The floorboards squeak and groan.

The windows are narrow and dust-smeared, and sunlight slants in at odd angles, never seeming to brighten the rooms. The house feels cold even under the brightest sunlight on the warmest summer days.

The furniture is heavy, old, and dark and covered in a

powdery layer of dust. Big iron candelabras hang on the cracked, stained walls, and a giant chandelier juts down from the ceiling of the front room like a fat, black insect.

I feel a chill every time I step inside. But all the equipment and wires and lights and digital high-def cameras and crew members scurrying around help remind me that it's a movie set, not a haunted mansion.

Delia and I stepped into the vast front room and let the cold air rush over us. My eyes adjusted slowly to the eerie darkness.

The dining room had been totally transformed into a movie set. A tall scaffold stretched high above the long table and held a catwalk jammed with lights and camera equipment. I saw two guys in denim overalls hoisting themselves up the narrow rope ladder to the catwalk.

Delia tripped over a clump of cables, and I caught her before she fell. Two crew members were setting the dining-room table. The clatter of china and silverware was drowned out by shouting voices. A boom mike swung over our heads. Digital cameras were being moved into place.

I saw our director, Les Bachman, arguing with two of the camera operators. Les waves his hands a lot when he talks and always seems frantic and angry. He's a big, blustery guy who wears big, loose sweatshirts and baggy, unwashed jeans and likes to bump you and invade your space when he talks to you. I've heard some crew guys call him Hurricane Les.

But everyone seems to like him and respect him. Mom

says he's the top horror director in Hollywood—mainly because he *horrifies* everyone who works for him. I told you, Mom is a riot.

"Claire, check it out." Delia elbowed me.

I followed her gaze. Annalee was on the far side of the room. She was cozying up to a tall, red-bearded crew member. She kept touching the front of his t-shirt and smoothing her hand on his shoulder as she talked. The guy seemed to like it. He had a big grin on his face.

Annalee spotted us, let go of the crew guy, and came running over. She was wearing a pink, very low-cut top over white shorts. She almost knocked me over, wrapping me in a hug. Like we were long-lost sisters or something.

"Isn't this exciting?" she gushed. "Can you believe it? We're in a movie?" She backed off, nodded at Delia, and straightened the top of her blouse, which was almost down to her waist.

"It's Lana's big scene today," I said. "But look at her. Does she look thrilled? Not."

Lana huddled by the catering table with her costar, Jeremy Dane, who plays Randy. She looked totally stressed. She kept flipping through the script, stabbing her finger at different lines. Jeremy had his arm around her waist and kept nodding his head solemnly.

"Jeremy keeps looking at me," Delia whispered. "I think he likes me."

I figured Jeremy just wanted to get away from Lana. But I didn't say anything to spoil Delia's fantasy.

"Jeremy is so sweet," Annalee said. "I just love him. He and I have so much in common."

Oh, wow. Please kill me now.

She squeezed my hand. She had to be the *touchiest* person on earth. "Claire, I've been texting you. About your birthday party. I want to help. What can I do? Why don't you come over, and we'll sit by the pool and toss ideas back and forth? I'd love that. I have all kinds of ideas for you."

Annalee, I don't even want to invite you to my party.

"Yeah. Thanks," I managed to say. I pulled my hand free from her grip. "My parents are planning most of it. It's going to be a huge deal. You know. Here at the studio."

Her face twisted into a pout. "But you'll let me know what I can do? I really want to be there for you, dear."

Thank you, dear.

I know I sound catty. But trust me. She's a terrible person. She'll cling to you like a leech if you let her get too close. Why do you think Delia hadn't said a word? She knows Annalee, too.

"I'm so *pumped*," Annalee said. "I've been practicing my screams. I'm getting really good at it. I practiced them with Jake last night."

My breath caught in my throat. "You were with Jake last night?"

She nodded. She had an evil grin on her face. She knew what she was doing to me. "He's so awesomely adorable ... isn't he?"

Now *I* wanted to scream.

It was going to be a day of a lot of screams. Les Bachman wanted to get something difficult out of the way. So he decided to shoot Cindy's horrifying murder first.

The writers wanted to improve the scene from the original script. In our version, the six teenagers are in the dining room. Randy and Tony get into a shoving match. They bump the dining-room sideboard. A sword falls from the ceiling and *slices Cindy in half.*

"Cutting off a hand is too tame for today's audiences," Les explained to us all during rehearsals. "These days, you have to slice a whole body." He shook his head. "Give the audience what it wants, right?"

Of course, it would be different from the original film. The slicing would all be done with CGI.

I shivered. It was freezing cold and damp inside the house. I wished I could pull on a sweatshirt or something, but I wasn't supposed to mess up my costume or my hair.

I raised my eyes past the catwalk to the high ceiling and saw the two crossed swords hovering over the long dining-room table. Seeing those swords made me shiver again. Nothing had changed in this house in sixty years.

And once again I saw the moment in the original movie when the sword dropped from the ceiling and cut off Cindy's hand. Cut it off so neatly. So cleanly . . . clean until her blood started to pump out like a fountain.

A horrible death. Right here. Right where Delia and Annalee and I were standing.

And we were about to do the scene all over again.

Delia gave me a gentle elbow poke. "Stop thinking grim thoughts," she said.

"Excuse me? Since when do *you* know what I'm thinking?"

"I could see the look on your face, Claire. Stop stressing. Everything's going to be okay this time. You've been listening to Jake too much. It's all going to be digital this time, right?"

I raised my eyes to the ceiling. "The swords are still up there, Dee. Lana is going to be sitting right under them."

"Get over yourself," she said. "History doesn't always repeat itself. This time, it'll all be fine."

"Places, actors," Les shouted. He waved us onto the set with both hands. "Look alive. This isn't a zombie movie. Yet!"

A few people laughed at his lame joke. We all hurried toward the dining-room table.

"Okay, let's set you in your places," Les said. "We'll block this out and try a few run-throughs."

Annalee stepped up to Les, fiddling with the top of her blouse. "Where am I, Les? Over by the end?"

Before Les could answer, I heard a man scream from above. "Hey—look out!"

I gazed up in time to see the sword fall. No time to move. It shot straight down. The long blade gleamed in my eyes— until it sliced down over Annalee.

"Noooooo!" I shut my eyes and opened my mouth in a screech of horror.

I raised my eyes to the ceiling. The two crisscrossed swords were still in place. My chest was heaving up and down. I gulped in large mouthfuls of air.

Delia held on to me. "Are you okay?"

"Yes," I choked out. "I thought—"

"I know what you thought," Delia said. "Claire, you've got to get your head in a better place. Really."

"But it could have *killed* her," I insisted.

Les broke in to our conversation. "Okay, go home, everyone. Just go home. I have to deal with this. I won't have this on my set. Go home. We've had enough horror for today."

Voices and cries of surprise all around.

"And don't start talking about the Curse of Mayhem Manor," Les warned. "That was a tech accident. That's all. I'm going to have a little meeting with these guys right now."

He waved with his clipboard. "Go on. Get out. Be back tomorrow at nine sharp." He gazed up at the catwalk. "We'll have some changes made. That won't happen again. I promise you, it'll be safe here from now on."

Delia and I turned to leave. Annalee trotted up to us. "Wow. That was scary. Like I didn't know what was happening, and then it was all over before I could even make a sound."

"Glad you're okay," I murmured.

"What a shame no one filmed it or videoed it or anything," she said. "I could be a star, right? At least on YouTube."

I saw Delia roll her eyes. "Annalee," she said, "is that all you think about? Being a star?"

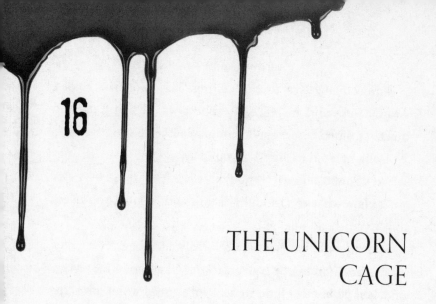

16

THE UNICORN CAGE

I HEARD A CRASH AND A SHATTER OF GLASS.

Someone grabbed me around the waist. I turned to see Delia holding on to me. "It's okay, Claire," she said softly. "It's okay."

"Huh?" I raised my eyes to Annalee. She stood beside Les. They were both staring down at the floor in front of them.

Shouts and cries erupted all over the set. Tense laughter. Crew guys moved quickly toward the table.

"Close call," someone said on the catwalk above us. "Sorry about that. A cable came loose. Everyone okay?"

A light had crashed down from the catwalk. The black metal case was on its side. The glass had shattered into a million pieces over the floor at Les's and Annalee's feet.

Not a sword. Annalee hadn't been sliced. A light. Not a sword. I had imagined . . . imagined . . .

She shook her head. "No. I think about guys, too."

Delia and I laughed. I'm not sure she meant it to be funny.

"Where are you two going?" she asked, stepping between us and putting an arm around each of our shoulders. "Can I hitch a ride?"

My family and Jake's family have dinner out together once a week. And we usually eat at The Ivy. There are a million restaurants in L.A., but everyone feels comfortable there, and our parents like to see all their buddies in the movie business.

A lot of young movie people and stars hang at Joan's on Third. But my parents still prefer The Ivy.

Jake and I always order the same thing—the fried calamari and the salami pizza. Jake's dad gives us a hard time. "It's a fine restaurant," he says. "It's not a pizza joint." But Jake and I happen to like the salami pizza. So give us a break.

Mr. Castellano is the only one who is tense at dinner. He's the one who jumps up from his chair and runs to say hi whenever someone he knows walks in. Jake's mom just sits and waves to them. And my parents always concentrate on their food. I think they're happy to let Jake's dad do all the work and schmooze with all the movie people and let them enjoy their dinner.

Tonight, we arrived at the same time. The valets took the cars, and we sat at our usual table outside near the door so Jake's dad could see who comes in and out. He was in his uniform—black Armani suit, pale blue shirt, and red tie. Jake's mom wore designer skinny jeans and a white sweater top, because she gets cold even in the summer.

The waiter came around and Dad ordered the usual, vodka martinis for everyone. "I'll have one, too," I said. "Extra olives, please." A joke. But they just stared at me, and I asked for a Sprite.

"How's the internship going with Zack?" Jake's dad asked him, arranging his silverware the way he likes it.

"Great," Jake said. "I'm learning a lot. He really knows the new software. Of course, we haven't really had anything to edit. I didn't go to the studio today."

"You missed all the excitement," I said.

Jake grinned. "I heard about it. The Curse of Mayhem Manor strikes again."

"Don't talk that way," his dad snapped. "I don't want any curse talk around here. This picture is very important to us all."

"Oops. Sorry." Jake didn't bother to make his apology sound sincere.

Mrs. Castellano checked her lipstick in a little hand mirror. "What did you do today instead of the studio?" she asked.

"Shawn came over and we hung out at the pool," Jake said.

His mom squinted at him. "Have you been drinking?"

"No. Of course not."

I almost burst out laughing. Jake smelled like a Budweiser factory. Did he really think he was fooling anyone?

His mom pressed her lips together. "I'm always surprised you and Shawn are such good friends. You really don't have much in common."

I knew she didn't approve of Shawn. She thought he was a bum.

"You know," Jake said, tapping his fork on the table, "the thing about Shawn? I've never been with Shawn when I didn't have a good time."

His mom blinked. "What's he doing this summer? He isn't doing anything at all, right?"

"Hey, give him a break," Jake said. "His parents just split. He's . . . adjusting, you know?"

Mrs. Castellano looked like she wanted to say more about Shawn, but the waiter came with a tray of martinis. My parents had been quiet the whole time. Dad had that faraway look in his eyes, like he had something serious on his mind.

He was dressed casual, in khakis, a pale yellow shirt, and a navy blazer. He clinked glasses with Mom and everyone said "Cheers." My mom used to act in a TV sitcom, and she's still pretty hot. For a mother, anyway.

She has frizzy, white-blond hair and big blue eyes, and wears very short skirts and tight t-shirts. She's totally hung up about looking young. She talks in a whispery, hoarse sitcom voice, and she's very funny.

I leaned across the table and whispered to Jake, "How's it going?"

He grinned and whispered back, "Shawn and I had a few beers, so I'm trying to act normal."

Like duh.

I snickered. "You? Act normal?"

"Whatever."

At the other end of the table, my mom was talking about a new designer store on Wilshire. She said, "It's so outrageously expensive, but at least they're rude to you." That's Mom. A laugh a minute.

The dads were shaking their heads and talking in low voices, something about Disney grosses. Or maybe about something that grossed them out. I couldn't really hear.

Dad suddenly turned to Jake and me. "*Mayhem Manor* is going to be huge," he said. "Doing a remake of a horror film that ended in real horror is *brilliant*."

"Sy, it was *your* idea," Mom told him.

"That's why it's brilliant!" he said.

Everyone laughed.

He took a sip of his martini. "It's going to save the studio. We've had nothing but flops. I can't tell you how much we're counting on this film. If it doesn't work, we won't be eating at The Ivy much longer."

Whoa. Heavy-duty.

"It's going to be a smash," my mom said. "It's going to be bigger than paste."

Everyone laughed again.

The waiter brought our first course. The four adults all had salads. Jake and I always split the fried calamari.

As I shoveled a bunch of them onto my plate, I studied Jake. His eyes seemed to be clearing. His cheeks had faded from bright red to pink. I wondered if he remembered the potion. If he remembered being so nasty to me.

And the question just burst from my mouth. You know how sometimes you don't mean to, but you say what you are thinking?

"Hey, what's the story about the little guy in the trailer?" I said.

Dad lowered his salad fork. The other three adults turned to me.

"What little guy?" Mr. Castellano asked.

"You know," I said. "The short little bearded guy with all the black hair? Looks like a bear cub? He's in that trailer right next to the wardrobe department. It's crammed with little bottles. He calls them his potions."

They stared at me. They didn't move or speak.

My dad and Mr. Castellano exchanged glances. The two women remained silent.

"Oh. Right," Dad said finally. "The trailer with all the potions."

"Do you know it?" I asked.

"Sure," he said. "It's right next to the cage where we keep the unicorn. You know. Across from Rudolph the Red-nosed Reindeer?"

Everyone had a good laugh at my expense.

"I'm serious, Dad," I said when everyone finally stopped laughing.

"Me, too," he said. "I'm serious, dear. There's no trailer next to wardrobe. And there's no little short bearded guy who gives out potions."

17

THE LAST NORMAL NIGHT

DAD HATES WHEN PEOPLE ARGUE at the dinner table. So I shut up about the trailer and the potions. I knew Dad was wrong. It's a big studio. He doesn't know everything that goes on there.

He *had* to be wrong, because I had been inside that trailer. And spoken to the hairy little creep. And stolen a potion and used it on Jake. Jake couldn't back me up because he had no memory of it. But Delia could.

They all love to laugh at me. They think I'm some kind of woo-hoo fantasy freak. Because I hear and see things they don't. Well, maybe I'm just more sensitive than other people.

I'm going back there, I decided. *And I'm going to get the right potion this time. The love potion. And I'm definitely going to use it on Jake.*

Unless I didn't have to. Unless I could make him see how I felt about him *without* having to sprinkle a potion on his head.

I gave him meaningful looks all through dinner. And I tried to channel Annalee. I kept touching him a lot. Squeezing his hand and patting his shoulder.

Mainly, I concentrated hard, sending him thought waves. I really believed if I kept sending my feelings on psychic waves directly to his brain, he would recognize them. He would understand.

I can't help it. I believe in magical things. I always have. You can't *imagine* how crushed I was when a kid in preschool told me Santa Claus was a fake. I was only four, but I really wanted to believe.

I beat up that kid in the sandbox. I mean, I really pounded him. I can still remember it. I made him eat sand. But I knew he was telling the truth.

So now I sent my psychic brain waves to Jake. He definitely was not getting them. At one point, he pulled a salami slice off his pizza and offered it to me. That was our tenderest moment.

After dinner, as we stood on the sidewalk waiting for the valets to bring around our cars, I decided to take action. I leaned forward and kissed his cheek.

He actually jumped. He nearly fell off the curb. He turned and squinted at me like I was from another planet.

"Oh. Sorry," I said. "Stumbled. It's these shoes. Not used to them."

He nodded. And wiped his cheek.

I could feel my face turning red. But I decided to press on. "Hey, you know the new club on Sunset? It's called The Club, and a lot of kids from school have been hanging there. Want to check it out tonight?"

He took a few seconds to think about it. "I don't think so," he said finally.

I made a pouty face. "Why not?"

"I've got a lot to do. Uh . . . Zack gave me some assignments. Some software things I have to work out."

I nodded. My heart was beating kind of fast all of a sudden. Not from excitement. From disappointment.

"Well, do you want to just hang out when you're finished with that?" I blurted out.

"Not tonight," he said. "Why? Did you want to talk to me about something?"

"No," I said. "Not really." The valet brought our BMW around, and I called good night to his parents and slumped into the backseat.

As he drove home, Dad was telling Mom about some producer from Fox he saw at the restaurant. Mom said she couldn't get over how fabulous Amy Castellano's skin is. "It's smooth as a cloudy day."

Huh?

I tuned them out and pulled my phone from my bag. It chimed. A text message.

Maybe Jake changed his mind, I thought.

But no. It was from Shawn. Asking me if I wanted to get together at his house.

Give up, Shawn.

I didn't know what to do about Shawn. I liked him, but I didn't really want to spend time with him. How could I get him to text Delia and not me?

I had another text from Annalee. The same old thing. She wanted to know if I wanted to come over and talk about my birthday party with her.

How about NEVER?

Of course, there was no way she could help out. I was planning the party with my parents. It was going to spread out over the whole movie studio. Mom and Dad said they wanted me to have the biggest, most fabulous Sweet Seventeen party ever. (Also, they wouldn't mind the press coverage for the studio.)

Staring at her text on the phone, I suddenly felt sorry for Annalee. She had some kind of fantasy that we were like best friends. Didn't she see I avoided her whenever I could? She made me tense. I could feel myself tighten up. I never could be myself around her.

How could any girl be her friend? She is so totally hung up on herself. And she is a slut, let's face it. No one's boyfriend is safe around her. I mean, I don't have to worry. I don't have a boyfriend. But if I did . . .

Anyway, I texted her back. Said I wanted to get my beauty rest for the shoot tomorrow.

When we got home, Maria, our housekeeper, greeted us in the kitchen in tears, talking in Spanish a mile a minute. She has a lot of family problems. Dad has been trying to bring her children up from Colombia, but he hasn't had much luck with the immigration people.

Mom led Maria into the den to try to calm her down. Dad stopped me as I started toward the stairs. "Want to come down to the screening room? I have some dailies to watch. You know. From *Please Don't*."

Please Don't is the romantic comedy Dad is making at the studio with another production company. It's about two young women in New York who get sick of their boyfriends and decide it would be fun to drive them crazy. Really. Like mental hospital crazy.

"I can't," I told him. "I have to call Delia." I could see the disappointment on his face. Watching dailies in our screening room downstairs is one of the ways Dad and I bond. "Maybe a movie later?" I said.

"Maybe. I have to do some budget stuff. But, maybe." I watched him head toward the basement stairs. He works too hard. Mom is able to turn it off when she gets home, but Dad just keeps going.

I climbed the stairs and turned on all the lights in my room. I guess it's neurotic, but I always have to have a lot of lights on. And I close my bedroom windows at night because of the jacaranda trees next door in Jake's backyard.

The trees are African. I don't know how Marty Castellano got them to his backyard. They smell sweet when they blossom, and their purple flowers are to die for. But they whisper at night.

This is not a joke, and I'm not a psycho nutcase. The

trees traveled a long way, and they brought strange magic of their homeland with them. At night, I can hear them whispering to one another. They whisper even when the air is still and there is no breeze.

And one night . . . very late one night when I couldn't sleep . . . I heard them whisper my name. I heard it so clearly. I froze. Every muscle froze. And lying under the covers, I listened to the whispers from across the yard . . .

Claire . . . Claaaaaaaaire . . .

I didn't scream but I wanted to.

I climbed out of bed and, on shaky legs, I crept to the open windows and closed them tight. And ever since that night, I keep the windows closed after dark. I turn up the air-conditioning and lock the windows and try not to think about the trees and how they knew my name.

Tonight I checked the windows and glanced over to Jake's house. His house was dark. The only light was in the kitchen. A pale half-moon made the whole world look silvery and unreal.

I pulled off my sneakers and sprawled on my bed. I pulled out my phone and punched Delia's number. She answered on the third ring. "Hey," I said. "I'm back from dinner."

I heard thumping music and a lot of voices. "Hi. What's up?" Delia had to shout.

"Where are you?" I asked.

"You know that new club?"

"The Club?"

"Yeah. I'm here with Jake."

"I can't hear you," I shouted. "It sounded like you said you were there with Jake."

Loud voices. Music pounding.

"Yeah. Jake. Can you hear me, Claire? I'm here with Jake."

My breath caught in my throat. I guess Jake didn't have software problems to work out after all. He sure didn't wait long to pick Delia up. But why did he lie to me? And why did Delia go out with him?

When I could finally breathe again, I blurted out: "Why?"

"Because I thought Shawn would be with him," Delia shouted into the phone.

"Is Shawn there?"

"No. He drove down to Laguna to see his dad. And so I'm stuck here with Jake." More music. Someone laughing really loud. "Claire, do you want to come down here and rescue me?"

"I don't think so. I'll catch you later."

"But, Claire—"

I clicked off.

I knew I shouldn't be pissed off at Delia. She just wanted to be with Shawn. But I felt way angry. Angry at Jake, I guess, for lying to me about how he had to work on an editing assignment. Angry at him for not wanting to take *me* to the club.

"It's messed up," I murmured, squeezing the phone as if I wanted to flatten it. "Just messed up. I'm going back to Puckerman, and I'm getting that love potion. This is just too messed up."

Of course, lying there staring up at the ceiling, I didn't realize how messed up life can get. I had no way of knowing that it was just normal life—and this was my last night of normal life.

The last night of normal life before all the horror began.

PART THREE

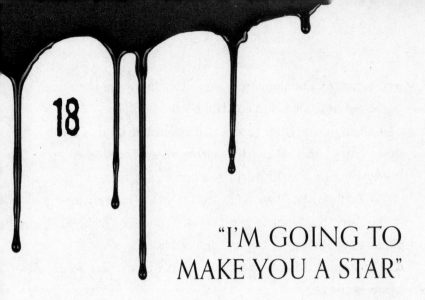

18

"I'M GOING TO MAKE YOU A STAR"

I DROVE TO THE STUDIO EARLY. I didn't wait for Delia. Rush-hour traffic to Burbank was like being in a zombie movie. I lurched forward a few feet at a time. But I was on a mission. I was determined to find Puckerman in his little trailer before I had to report to the set.

I parked the car in the employees' lot and trotted toward the wardrobe building. It was a hazy cool day, wisps of low fog clinging to the shrubs along the soundstage walls.

Dad is wrong, I told myself. *That trailer has to be there.*

And it was.

I had to squint to see it. It was almost hidden behind the morning mist and the shadow of the building wall.

My heart started to pound. I took a deep breath, then I grabbed the door, swung it open, and stepped inside. I blinked under the dim light on the ceiling. The shelves came into focus. As I remembered, they stretched from the floor to the ceiling, filled with colorful bottles and jars.

And there the little runt was. Puckerman sat in a black desk chair at the back of the narrow room. He jumped up, his dark eyes wide with surprise when he saw me.

"Claire," he said, "I wasn't expecting you. What a surprise."

My breath caught in my throat. "You—you're here," I choked out.

He scratched his heavy beard. "But why are *you* here?" he demanded.

I just came out and said it. "You told me you have a love potion. Right?"

He blinked his watery frog eyes. He picked at something on the front of his mesh t-shirt. "Sure, I have a love potion. But not for you."

"Please," I said. "If you—"

"I'll be calling you soon," he said. "You weren't supposed to remember me. I guess I didn't use enough of the forgetting potion."

I ignored him. I was determined to get what I came for. "The love potion," I said. "Does it work like you said? Really? I can pay you for it. Really. Does it work?"

"It isn't for you," he said, moving toward me. "You don't need a love potion, Claire. You don't have time."

His words made my breath catch in my throat. "Don't have time? What do you mean?"

"I'm going to need you. Soon," he said. "I don't want you to come here again until I call for you. I want you to forget."

He had a potion bottle in his hand. He dove toward me and raised it over my head.

I ducked my head and squirmed out of his reach. He stumbled into the trailer wall.

My eyes swept over the glittery bottles on the shelf beside me. I spotted the gray sparkly love potion. I grabbed it quickly, blocking Puckerman's view with my body. I tucked it into my pocket.

Puckerman swung around and tried again. He stabbed his hand toward me and shook black flakes from his bottle.

But I darted to the door. I pushed it open with my shoulder and stumbled outside.

"Stay away!" Puckerman shouted after me. "Stop thinking about the love potion, Claire. I have bigger plans for you. I'm going to make you a *star*."

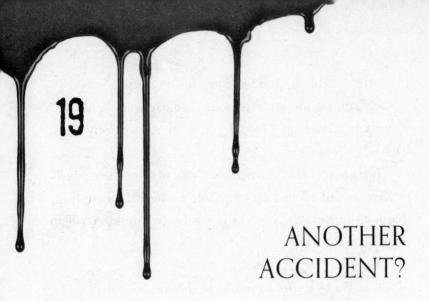

19

ANOTHER
ACCIDENT?

I STEPPED INTO MAYHEM MANOR, made my way to the dining-room set, and glanced around for Delia. I saw crew guys moving lights on the catwalk. A line of people were getting coffee at the catering table. I didn't see her there.

A hand grabbed my wrist. I turned to see Lana deLurean. Her blond hair was piled high in a bun, '60s-style. She had a lot of dark makeup around her blue eyes. She wore a very short red miniskirt and a yellow midriff-baring top that appeared to be made of shiny vinyl.

"Have you seen Pablo?"

"Good morning to you, too, Lana," I said.

My sarcasm went right by her. "I've been looking for him everywhere. He promised to go over the scene with me. This is my big scene, you know. Where I get murdered."

She didn't let go of my wrist. Her cold, bony hand was cutting off my circulation.

"I think Pablo is afraid to come inside," I said.

She sniffed for some reason. "Pablo is very sensitive," Lana said, frowning. "Would you help me with my lines, Delia?"

"I'm Claire," I said. "Remember? My dad owns the studio?"

She shoved a rolled-up script into my hands. "I have trouble with names. It's a learning disability. Would you help me, Claire?"

I nodded. "Well . . . sure."

"It might be useful to you, too," she added.

I doubted that. All I had to do in this scene was scream my guts out.

Lana pulled me to a corner away from the lights. Behind us, Les was arguing with a young, blond-haired man about a candelabra on the dining-room table. "It's ruining my shot," Les screamed. "Why do I want to see a candelabra? Whoever encouraged you to be a set designer? Your mother?"

"I could take it away," the guy said softly, calmly. Everyone was already used to Hurricane Les.

"Yes, you could do that," Les said, "or you could *sit* on it." The candelabra quickly vanished.

Lana grabbed my shoulder and turned me toward her. "Hurry. Don't watch them. We don't have much time, Delia."

I didn't bother to correct the name this time. It was obvious she never intended to get it right.

She shoved the rolled-up script at me. I grabbed for it but dropped it.

Lana muttered something under her breath. As I bent to

pick it up, I saw Delia and Annalee standing together on the other side of the dining-room table. I lifted the script and straightened the pages. "Where's the scene?" I asked Lana.

"This one. This one." Lana poked the page impatiently with a long red fingernail. "I'm sitting at the table. I say something about how we have to find dinner. The others are all arguing about how we're going to spend the night in this horrible house. Tony and Randy get into a fight . . ."

"Okay." My eyes scanned the page till I found the scene. Behind me, crew members were scurrying about. A boom mike was moved till it hovered over the table. More lights came on from the catwalk above. I heard Les shout that he was going to film the run-through, just in case it was good.

"Give me my first line," Lana demanded, squeezing my wrist. "Hurry. You're too slow. You're not being helpful at all." She gazed around frantically. "Where is Pablo? I can't believe that bald-headed rat is doing this to me."

"Jeremy, nice of you to show up," I heard Les say with total sarcasm.

I glimpsed Jeremy Dane stepping onto the set. He flashed Les his fabulous smile. He's twenty-three, boyish good looks to die for, a major tween-god and gossip mag idol from starring in *Whoa, Jeremy,* a Nickelodeon sitcom that rocked the TV ratings for six years. This is his first movie.

"Where've you been?" Les demanded. "You go out for a smoke?"

"I don't smoke," Jeremy replied.

"Well, maybe you should take it up. It might wake you up."

Jeremy shrugged. "Whatever." He smoothed a hand through his blond hair and flashed Lana a grin and a two-fingered salute. I saw Annalee hurry over to greet him.

"My first line," Lana said through gritted teeth. "Give it to me. What is it?"

"Uh ... you sit down at the table. And you say, 'Come on, guys. Let's all sit down. We can discuss it calmly. We have to go with the flow, right?' "

"That's too much. Go slower," Lana snapped. "Tony and Randy start arguing, right? There's a shoving match. What do I say? Where do I look? Quick—what do I say?"

Was she so nervous she forgot *everything*? Or was she pretending she needed all this help just for attention?

My guess was she wanted attention. I knew she wasn't stupid. She had spent the whole week of rehearsals pretending she needed everyone's help. But it was easy to see how phony that was.

I lowered my eyes to the script. "You shout at the two boys to stop fighting. Then you look up. You see the sword falling from the ceiling. I mean, you have to *pretend* you see it falling. You scream—"

"I know. I know," Lana snapped. "You don't have to tell me *everything*. I'm a professional, you know." She fluffed a hand up through her hair. "Okay. What do I do next?"

I opened my mouth to answer, but Les interrupted. "Places!" he called. "Everyone. Places. That means you, too, Lana. I see you hiding in the corner."

"I wasn't hiding," Lana replied sharply. "I was rehearsing." She went storming toward the dining-room set.

"Then you'll probably nail it in one take," Les said.

Lana flashed him her warmest, phoniest smile. "I always do my best for you, Les, dear."

"Well, you might start out on the other side of the table where you belong," Les said.

The crew members knew better than to laugh. But I saw a big grin spread over Jeremy Dane's face.

The studio publicity staff wanted to start a story that Jeremy and Lana had become a couple. But it wasn't true. Jeremy spent a lot of time huddling with Lana, playing nice with her and trying to help her with her part. But he was always making faces behind her back.

Les guided Lana to the edge of the set. "You enter from here and you walk to the chair in the middle. It's marked. See the tape on the back?"

Lana nodded. "No problem."

"You gaze up and down the table. You're a little worried. The six of you are spending the night in this haunted house, and no one is behaving well. You pull out the chair and sit down. Then you do your first line."

"I get it, Les."

"And don't look up at the swords. Not till I give the signal."

"Got it."

"When you see the sword shooting down, we have to see the horror on your face. Instant terror."

"Okay. No problem. But nothing really falls down on me?"

"We do that all later in CGI," Les said. "Nothing falls on you. But you have to see it in your mind, Lana. You have to see it crashing down on you."

"Of course, Les."

"Sit down," Les said. "Let's start with you sitting at the table. You know your lines, right?"

Lana pulled out the chair, then settled onto it. She hesitated. Then she called to me. "Delia, could you bring me my script? Could I have it back, please?"

I hadn't moved from the corner. I didn't even realize I still had the script in my hand. I took off running with the script raised in front of me. "Here it is," I called.

I was only a few feet from Lana when I tripped over a floor cable. I stumbled forward with my arm raised—and before I could catch myself, my head bumped the hard wood edge of the dining-room table.

"Owwww." I actually saw stars.

Shaking off the pain, I pulled myself to my feet. I heard alarmed voices all around. "I'm okay," I shouted. "Really."

But I heard a whisper in my ears. Like a gust of wind. Or a human sigh.

I pressed my hand over my forehead. The pain was fading but the whisper grew louder.

I glanced up—and my breath caught in my chest as I saw the swords on the ceiling move. They both tilted, up then down. One of the swords started to fall.

I froze. No time to move. No time to scream a warning.

The silvery blade came sailing straight down. Glowing in the lights, it fell straight like a guillotine blade.

I heard a sick *crunch*.

Lana's eyes bulged.

She raised her arm. And I saw...I saw...*no hand* attached to it. No hand. No hand on her wrist.

The blade sliced her hand off cleanly.

She opened her mouth to scream, but only a hoarse gagging sound escaped her throat.

A gusher of bright-red blood came spurting up from her open wrist. It splashed over the table and puddled on her lap.

The whole room exploded with cries and shouts. People sobbed and moaned in horror.

I tightened my jaw, struggling to keep my breakfast down.

And I stared at the small, pale hand all by itself on the table.

The fingers...

The fingers curled and uncurled.

The hand had been sliced off, but *the fingers still moved.*

The fingers rubbed the table. Clenched and unclenched.

And then they lay still.

20

DON'T DO IT, DELIA

LANA'S SCREAMS RANG OFF THE WALLS. People rushed to help her. Someone wrapped a towel around her arm to stop the blood spurting from her open wrist. Over her screams, I heard sirens outside. Security guards had gotten the word and came rushing in, looking alert and frightened, hands on their holsters.

I held my head, still throbbing from my stumble. The whispering in my head had stopped but the memory of it lingered. In the corner of the room, I saw the actor who plays Brian bent over, throwing up loudly.

I spotted Jake, hanging back by the doorway. I ran to him, my chest heaving, sobs shaking my body. I ran into his arms. I nearly knocked him over.

"Was it *my fault*?" The words burst out. "Did I do that? My head ... it bumped the table and then the sword crashed down."

Jake kept his arms around me. "It wasn't your fault," he said, eyes on the crew people stretching Lana out on the floor. Dark blood puddled under the table and her chair. Her screams had turned to moans.

"How could it be your fault, Claire?" Jake said. "Bumping the table didn't make that sword fall."

"Then . . . what did?" I gasped. "What did?"

Messed up. It was all messed up. A week later, we were all still totally freaked. The production was shut down. In fact, the whole studio had been abandoned while the police did their thing.

We were all at my house. Shawn, Delia, Jake, and me. We were spread out on the green leather chairs and the long couch in the den. There were Cokes and bowls of Tostitos and pretzels on the low slate coffee table. But no one felt like eating.

We tried to talk about other things, but it was hard because we all couldn't stop thinking about what had happened. Especially Jake, Delia, and me, who saw the whole thing.

"Every time I shut my eyes, I see the blood," I said. "It just came spraying out of her wrist . . . spurt . . . spurt . . . spurt . . . like from a pump. And then she started screaming. Screaming in this weird animal voice. You know. Like some creature being squeezed in a trap. And each scream came with another spurt of blood."

I covered my face with my hands. "I . . . just can't get the picture out of my mind. Or the sound of those horrible screams."

Shawn tried to put his arm around me. To comfort me, I guess. But I shrugged him away. He looked a little shocked at the rejection. But I didn't want to give him the wrong idea. He lumbered over to the foosball game in the corner of the room and fiddled with the handles.

Delia dropped beside me on the couch and took my hand. "I honestly didn't think it was real," she said, shaking her head. "I mean, we were making a movie, right? So my brain just figured it was part of the film. Special effects. Fake blood. Then . . . when I realized what was happening . . . that it was all *real* . . . I . . . I don't remember exactly. I must have shocked out or something."

Delia swallowed. I saw big teardrops cover both of her eyes. They rolled down her pale cheeks. "I kind of fell," she said. "I remember I dropped to my knees. I fell to the floor and covered my eyes. I didn't want to see it. That hand on the table by itself. Like a pale, white crab. I didn't want to see it. But I couldn't shut out the screams. I couldn't . . ."

Her voice trailed off. The two of us huddled together. Behind us, Shawn fiddled quietly with the foosball game. I knew he wasn't good at showing any emotion. A silence fell over the room.

I think we all jumped when the doorbell rang. Through the den doorway, I saw Maria, our housekeeper, hurrying to answer the front door.

A few seconds later, Annalee Franklin appeared. She was wearing yellow short shorts as tight as her skin, a tight sleeveless purple t-shirt, and purple sneakers to match. Her shiny black hair came down to her bare shoulders.

"I just came from the hospital," she said. She tossed her red vinyl bag against the side of the couch and dropped down next to Jake. She patted his leg. "Hey, Jake."

I jumped to my feet. "You saw Lana? I didn't think she was seeing anyone."

Annalee shrugged. "They let me in. I said I was family."

Family? Really?

"Well, how *is* she?" I asked. "Tell us. Don't keep us in suspense, Annalee. Is she okay? Is she getting out of the hospital?"

Annalee's expression turned serious. "She's not exactly okay. I mean, she lost so much blood, you know. She almost died. They didn't think she was going to make it."

"But she's okay now?"

"Well, she's going to live. But she . . . well . . . she wouldn't talk to me. She said I'm a stranger. She doesn't know me. I said I came to represent the whole cast. She just repeated the word. *Represent? Represent?* Then she turned her head to the wall. I think she's totally depressed."

"Of *course* she's depressed!" Delia exclaimed. "Wouldn't *you* be? Her career is over. She's finished. Toast. And all because of a stupid accident."

"It wasn't an accident," Jake said, turning to Delia. "I told you. It's the curse. The Curse of Mayhem Manor."

"Stop saying that," Delia scolded him. "That's just junk."

"How could it be an accident?" Jake said. "It was an exact copy of what happened in the original film. In that old film, Cindy got her hand sliced off. And now—what? Cindy got her hand sliced off. Do you really think that's just a coincidence? There's a curse on this film. Believe me."

I sighed. "Maybe Jake is right."

Delia scowled. "We don't need that superstitious garbage now. All your woo-hoo magic. This is real life. Real life."

"Maybe it's not superstitious garbage," I told her. I grabbed Delia's arm. "I heard something, Delia. Just before the sword came crashing down. I heard a whisper . . . a loud whisper in my ears and . . . and it sounded *human*."

"Stop it, Claire. Just stop it," Delia begged. She covered her ears.

"Even Pablo, Lana's psychic, warned her not to go in the old house," I said. "He felt the curse, too."

Annalee had her hand on Jake's thigh. I wanted to kill her. She kept leaning against him. Teasing him.

"They're going to go on with our film, right?" she asked me. "Did your dad say—"

I sighed again. "Dad says the lawyers want to stop production. Lana's going to have a major lawsuit, and—"

"But our parents are counting on this film," Jake interrupted. "They need this movie to keep the studio going. They really want to start up again as soon as the police finish in the old house."

A wave of sadness rolled over me. "I've waited so long for this break. Years! I really hope we can keep filming."

Shawn stepped away from the foosball game and sat

down in the chair across from Annalee. He was staring at her legs. "In the hospital, did you see Lana's arm?" he asked her.

"It's all wrapped up. It has like a cast over it."

"It looks like a stump?" Shawn asked.

"Don't be gross," I said. "What do you *think* it looks like?"

Shawn shrugged. "Just asking."

"Let's try to change the subject," Annalee said. "Tell us about your birthday party, Claire. Why are you making such a big deal over seventeen?"

I really didn't want to discuss my party with her. But maybe it would help get us out of this deep muck of sadness.

"Because I couldn't have a Sweet Sixteen," I said. "No one was around last year." I shook my head. "That's why having your birthday in the summer is the *worst*. Everyone's always away."

"You were away, too," Annalee said. "Your family was in France, remember? Remember how I begged you to take me along?"

"Anyway, that's why they promised me I could have a *huge* Sweet Seventeen," I said. "They said I can have the whole studio . . . anyone I want to invite . . . bands . . . lights . . . food trucks . . ."

"Wow. I'm ready to party!" Annalee said. She flashed Jake a smile and rubbed her hand on his arm. She was definitely coming on to him—right in front of me, even though she knew how I felt about Jake.

I decided to ignore it. "They said I could have anything I could dream up," I continued. "So I'm calling it A Midsummer Night's Dream. We all read the play last year, right? It's going to be like that, with fairies and lights in the trees and all kinds of magic and music all night."

"Awesome," Shawn said. "Did they have Coors in Shakespeare's time?"

"For sure," Jake said. "But no coolers. So they had to drink it warm."

Annalee laughed as if Jake had made the funniest joke in history and pressed her forehead against his shoulder.

Dad walked into the room. He had a serious look on his face. He had just come from the studio. He was still dressed in khakis, a blue dress shirt and tie, and his navy blazer.

"We got the go-ahead from the lawyers," he announced.

"You mean . . . you're going ahead with the picture?" I said.

He nodded.

I wanted to jump up and cheer. I saw Delia's eyes flash with excitement.

"Maybe some of you would like to quit," Dad said, his eyes stopping on each one of us. "That would be okay. You just have to tell me now. If you believe like Claire that there's a curse on the film—"

"Wait a minute," I cried, jumping to my feet. "*Jake* is the one who thinks there's a curse. And now that the same thing happened to Lana that happened to that girl back in 1960—"

Dad raised a hand to cut me off. "I know. Do you think we haven't discussed the whole thing for days? It was a terrible, terrible accident. And I know your take on it, Claire. I know you think there's some kind of evil supernatural curse on the house and—"

I scowled at him. "You're making fun of me. It's like a joke to you?"

"Believe me, it's no joke," Dad said. He turned to Jake. "Your parents agree with me, Jake. We're all in agreement. We have come through a terrible tragedy. But if we want our studio to survive, we need the film to go on."

Jake shrugged in reply. "I'm just an intern," he muttered. "I'll stick with it if everyone else will." Annalee squeezed his hand.

Dad turned to Delia. "We have to replace Lana," he said, rubbing his chin. "We decided we don't have time to go out and find another well-known actress. So we thought of you, Delia. You're beautiful and you've acted in other productions. And you've been in rehearsals, so you're familiar with the part. Will you step into the starring role for us?"

I don't know about the others. But I just stared at Delia, who had her hands pressed to the sides of her face and looked totally shocked. And I thought: *Don't do it, Delia. Please don't do it. Something terrible could happen. Please don't be next.*

"Of course I'll do it," Delia said. "Thanks."

21

PUCKERMAN
REFLECTS

THE NEXT DAY, DELIA HAD a craving for cupcakes, and when Delia has a craving, there's no talking to her until she satisfies it. I mean, if you've ever seen a totally insane crazed person, you know what Delia can be like. Even about cupcakes.

So I drove her to Crumbs on Little Santa Monica. She had a red velvet and I had a plain yellow with coconut icing. I don't really understand the fuss about cupcakes. Why not go all the way and have a slice of cake?

But Delia barely spoke as she washed down big hunks of the red velvet with a cappuccino (two sugars). Then she took her finger, picked up cupcake crumbs off the tabletop with it, and ate them, too.

Finally, she smiled. "Claire, what about your Sweet Seventeen? Did your dad say it was still okay to have it at the studio?"

I nodded. "Yeah. No problem. He said he wants to show the studio off. Show everyone having a good time there. You know. Make them forget about what happened to Lana."

Delia snickered. "It'll be awesome. Did you catch the jealous look on Annalee's face when you started talking about your party? She acted real gung-ho, but she was totally jealous."

I poked at the cupcake on my plate. "Where did she have *her* party last year? At that rave club on Sunset?"

"Yeah. You missed it. You were away. Half the kids puked their guts out from some bad vodka drink her friend Angel sneaked in."

Delia picked up my cupcake off my plate and finished it. "Annalee said she wanted to hook up with sixteen guys for her Sweet Sixteen. But I don't think she achieved it since the guys were all puking."

"Annalee likes to brag."

"Annalee is a slut."

"That's harsh," I laughed. "But true."

Delia had her eyes on the front counter. "Want to split another one? German chocolate cake?"

"I don't have your metabolism, Delia. I put on five pounds by being in the same zip code as a cupcake."

"I always get starving when I'm stressed," she said.

"You know me," I said. "I'm a Häagen-Dazs freak when I'm nervous. I go right for the Caramel Cone or the Dulce de Leche."

"I can't believe your dad wants me to star in the film,"

Delia said, playing with a thick strand of her black hair. "I mean, what is he thinking? Sure, I've done modeling, but I've never had a speaking role—"

"You'll be awesome," I said. "There aren't many lines to learn. You just have to scream a lot and look fabulous."

She stared hard at me. I knew what she was thinking. Sometimes best friends can read each other's thoughts. She was thinking about Lana. Thinking about the sword dropping so fast and that sick *slicing* sound as it cut off Lana's hand.

"The curse thing. It's over," I said. "The worst possible thing has already happened. So, no more bad things to come. You'll see. It'll be totally smooth from now on."

"Jeremy Dane wants to meet with me," she said.

I blinked. "Really?"

"He says we should get to know each other before we start filming."

"That's awesome. When?" I asked.

She glanced at her watch. "Uh . . . now. I guess I'm late."

My mouth dropped open. "Jeremy Dane is a total star. And you stood him up?"

"I didn't stand him up, Claire. I'm just late. I . . . didn't want him to think I'm too eager."

I groaned. "Maybe he didn't want to jump you. Maybe he just wanted to make you feel more comfortable working with him."

She shrugged. "Whatever. You know his reputation. You read the magazines, too. He—"

"Those magazines all lie, Delia. They trash everybody." I

climbed out of the booth. "Come on. Let's go to Burbank. Maybe you can still catch him."

I had to pull her out of the booth. She studied her reflection in the window glass. "My hair . . ."

"Looks great," I said. "Let's go." I led the way to my mom's white Volvo, parked at the end of the block. We climbed in and I started it up.

Delia turned the mirror toward her and studied herself. She pulled lip gloss from her bag and smoothed it carefully over her lips. "Claire, do me a favor?"

"What favor?"

"Come with me. You come meet Jeremy Dane, too."

"But he doesn't want—"

"Please?"

I'd always thought Delia had a lot more self-confidence than me. I thought it came with being a total knockout. But, you learn things about people when they're stressed.

"Sure. Okay," I said. "Where are you meeting him?"

"At the commissary."

We made pretty good time to Burbank. Traffic was backed up on Cahuenga, but once I turned off, we bombed along. I waved to Ernesto, the guy at the studio gate, and we pulled into the exec parking lot.

Delia stretched her arms over her head as we climbed out of the car. It was a warm, clear day. The air was cool and fresh. A day to be happy to live in L.A. And the magic of being in a movie studio always swept over me as soon as I walked onto the lot.

The streets were quiet. We passed Soundstage A, where they were filming the comedy *Please Don't*. Empty and silent. They were probably away on location. And the *Mayhem Manor* cast wasn't due till this afternoon.

I heard a few voices from the open commissary window. "Maybe Jeremy is still there," I said. I rolled my eyes. "You're only an hour late."

Delia bit her bottom lip. "I know. I had to choose between Jeremy and a cupcake and . . ." Her voice trailed off.

I pulled open the front door, held it for Delia, and we stepped into the front hall. The aroma of eggs, bacon, toast, and grilled ham washed over us. They were still serving breakfast. From down the hall, I heard the clatter of silverware and someone laughing loudly.

The hall leading to the dining room was mirrored on both sides. Delia stopped to check herself out. She brushed her hair down with both hands. She tugged the short pleated skirt down over her tights.

I walked a few steps in front of her. My chest felt kind of fluttery. I guess I was nervous, too. I glimpsed myself in the mirror. Then I stopped suddenly—and gasped.

That dark, bearded face. Grinning at me from the mirror.

I recognized him at once. Benny Puckerman.

His eyes, his nasty grin, reflected clearly in the mirror.

I spun around to face him. "Huh?"

He wasn't there.

I turned back to the mirror. I gazed from wall to wall.

The little hair ball grinned at me from mirrors on both

sides of the hall. He raised two hairy fingers to his forehead and gave me a salute.

I stopped breathing. My mouth dropped open. I felt a wave of cold run down my body.

I turned again. He wasn't there. He wasn't in the hall. So how could he be reflected in the mirrors?

"Delia," I gasped. "Delia—look."

But the mirror reflected only my frightened face. Puckerman was gone.

22

JEREMY IS NEXT

MY HEART WAS POUNDING A MILE A MINUTE. I still felt cold all over. I kept my eyes on the mirrors as I followed Delia into the dining room.

I kept expecting Puckerman to pop back into view with that ugly grin. But he didn't reappear. My head was spinning. How did he do that? Was it some kind of trick? Was he deliberately trying to scare me?

Delia was chattering about how she couldn't believe she was actually going to be talking with Jeremy Dane and how stupid she was to keep him waiting. She always chatters away when she's nervous.

I wasn't listening. My brain was fried. I was trying to make sense of what I'd just seen and, of course, I couldn't.

Sunlight poured down from a big skylight in the ceiling. Three or four tables were filled with studio people, mostly crew members. A waitress was collecting plates, stacking them on one arm in an incredible balancing act. I saw Ace, the black-and-white dog from the comedy picture, sitting at a table like a human. He had a bowl of raw hamburger in front of him. Two women and a white-haired man in a dark suit shared his table.

Delia grabbed my shoulder and pointed. "There he is. He's still here."

Jeremy Dane sat in the back corner, reading his phone. A fruit plate sat uneaten in front of him. He held a white coffee mug in his free hand.

"Oh, wow," Delia murmured. She squeezed my shoulder.

"Relax," I said. Then I said, "Don't you hate it when people tell you to relax?"

That made her laugh.

We made our way through the room to Jeremy's table. He didn't look up as we approached. He was concentrating hard on his phone. His straight blond hair fell over his forehead. He wore a black t-shirt and black jeans. A tiny diamond stud flashed in one ear.

"Hi," Delia said, stepping up to the table. I hung a few feet back. "Sorry I'm late."

Jeremy raised his eyes from his phone and brushed the hair off his forehead. He had big brown cow eyes that made him look very serious. "Are you late? I was concentrating." He raised his phone.

"You were texting?" Delia said.

He shook his head. "No. Look." He turned the screen around. "It's the script of another project I might do."

"Cool," Delia said.

We were both standing awkwardly in front of the table. "I'm Claire," I said. "I'm Delia's friend. I'm in the film, too."

"I saw you on the set," he said. His smile was kind of lopsided—but sexy.

He motioned for us to sit down. Delia pulled out the chair across from him. But before she could sit down, I saw Ace leap off his chair and come running over to us. The dog's tail was whipping back and forth excitedly, and he jumped up on Delia.

Delia let out a startled cry. She tried to brush the dog away with both hands. Ace hopped on his back legs, still jumping on Delia. "They know when you don't like dogs," Delia said, struggling with Ace. "Dogs always come to me because they know I don't like them."

I dove for the dog, wrapped my hands around his middle, and hoisted him off the floor. He was startled at first, but then he turned his head and licked my cheek.

The white-haired man in the dark suit came over to take the dog from me. "Sorry about that," he said to Delia.

"I'm fine. Really," she replied. "I'm so embarrassed. I just have a thing about dogs. A phobia, I guess."

She turned to Jeremy. "A huge dog knocked me down and bit me when I was two. I've been afraid of dogs ever since. I just can't help it."

Jeremy snickered. He was watching the man across the room. The man scolded Ace, then set him back down in his chair. "Whoa. That dog is a cute dude. You should deal with your phobia, you know?"

Delia blushed. "I've tried," she said softly.

I expected Jeremy to say something nice. You know. Something to make Delia feel better. But he didn't.

"You like horror films?" he asked, gazing from her to me.

Before we could answer, the waitress interrupted. "Get you ladies anything?"

Delia and I ordered coffees. "And how about a plate of biscotti?" Jeremy said. The waitress nodded. "And you can refresh my coffee." He waved his mug in her face.

She grabbed the mug and walked away. Jeremy studied his phone for a moment. Then he turned back to us. "This film is weird, huh? I'm just doing it to fill in. I've got a Tim Burton thing working, and my agent is talking to Wes Anderson. You know who they are, right?"

Does he think we're from Mars? Does he think he has to impress us?

He was doing a pretty bad job.

"I think everyone is going to be a little shaky getting back to the set," I said. "I mean . . . after the accident."

His big eyes flashed. "They called me this morning from *Entertainment Weekly*. They wanted to ask me about the sword thing. They asked me what happened to Lana's hand. They asked if anyone kept it."

"Ohh, sick," Delia said.

Jeremy laughed. "Yeah. Pretty much."

"What did you tell them?" I asked.

"I said I keep it in my back pocket to remind me of her." He burst out laughing. Delia and I didn't join in.

Heat floated up from the pavement as we walked to the back of the lot.

I was happy to step into the shade of Mayhem Manor. The air instantly grew cooler. It took a few seconds for my eyes to adjust to the darkness as we stepped inside.

"Where is everyone?" Delia's voice sounded hollow in the empty front room.

I heard voices somewhere in the back. And then a crash. Someone laughed. Not serious.

Delia and I followed the voices past the dining room, now dark and deserted. I glanced at the tabletop. The blood stains had all been removed.

We stepped into the kitchen. Crew members struggled to prop up a light pole that had fallen. Other workers dusted and fussed and moved items around on the stove and counter.

When he saw us enter, Les Bachman turned away from Lazslo, the cinematographer, closed his notebook, and came hurrying over. "Good morning, ladies. Are you ready to rock and roll?"

Delia and I nodded. "We weren't sure if you were filming today or just rehearsing," I said.

"Full speed ahead," Les said, with unusual enthusiasm. What happened to his grouchy personality? Was he pretending to be energetic and up to get us back in the mood to work?

Annalee came walking over from behind the kitchen counter. She was already in costume. A silky fuchsia midriff-baring top with fringe and tight jeans. "How's it going?"

What a sensitive guy.

"I know I'm going to be kind of stressed going back in the mansion," Delia said. "How about you?"

"I'll definitely keep my hand off the dining-room table," Jeremy said. He laughed again.

The waitress brought our coffee and set down a plate of biscotti. Jeremy grabbed two off the plate before anyone else had a chance.

"We watched the original film," I told him. "You know. From 1960."

That caught his attention. His smile faded. He squinted at me, stirring his coffee. "Really? You did? You saw it? Is it any good?"

"It's hard to say," Delia answered. "You know it never got finished."

He crunched a chocolate biscotti in his teeth. "I know."

"The girl who played Cindy in the film sat at the dining-room table, and a sword dropped down and cut off her hand," I said. "For real. It killed her. She bled to death. And the camera kept rolling. Delia and I watched her die. It was *horrible.*"

Jeremy stopped chewing. "So the same thing happened *twice?*"

I nodded.

"Sweet!" Jeremy exclaimed, pounding the table. "Can you imagine the media blast we're going to get from that?"

A burst of anger swept over me. My hand trembled, and I spilled some coffee onto the table. "You know, Lana is a person," I snapped. "Her career was *ruined* by that sword. Her *life* is ruined."

Jeremy brushed back his hair. "I didn't really know her," he said. He took another bite of biscotti. Then he said something very strange. "You know, you can only die once."

Delia and I exchanged glances. I knew we were both thinking the same thing: *Is he the coldest, most insensitive jerk we've ever met?*

"Think about it," he said.

What is he talking about?

He checked his phone and tapped a reply to someone. Then I could see a thought strike him. "Hey, my scene is next. You watched the old movie. What happens to *me*?"

"You get pushed through a garbage disposal," I said. Oops. A little hostile maybe. But this dude was making me angry.

He swallowed. "Really?"

"Joke," I said.

"You get electrocuted by a toaster," Delia told him. "You want to make a sandwich. But you get zapped by the toaster."

Jeremy let out a breath. "Guess I should read the script. Wow." He rubbed his perfect nose. "I usually just wing it, you know. I get the flavor of the script. Then I do my own thing with it. It's a lot more natural that way." He turned to Delia. "You take classes with Klausen?"

"Who?"

He snickered. "Guess you don't. Klausen taught me a lot about going with my own thing. You know. Follow my gut

feelings. Use the script as a jumping-off point. Then *beco* the character in my own words."

He patted Delia's hand. He was staring at her boo "You should study with him. He likes brunettes."

What does that mean, exactly?

He kept his hand over Delia's. His dark eyes flashed. brought his face close to hers. "Maybe you and I could wo together on it later. I could show you Klausen's techniqu think it would help you."

Was he coming on to her? Or insulting her? Hard to te

I glanced at the time on my phone. "We should get to t set." I scooted my chair back.

Jeremy fumbled in his back pocket. "Guess I left my w: let in the dressing room," he said. "Can one of you take ca of the check?"

Jeremy said he had some things to take care of, so Delia ar I walked to Mayhem Manor. It gave us a chance to dis Mainly to agree on how much we disliked Jeremy Dane.

"It's good that he likes *himself* so much," Delia said, "be cause no one else could."

"Maybe his mom likes him," I said.

"Why would she?" Delia replied.

I searched my bag for those Ray-Bans Dad had given me Then I remembered I'd left them in the wardrobe buildin, and never went back to get them. The sun was killer today

"Good," Delia and I answered in unison.

"Have you seen the gorgeous Jeremy?" Les asked.

"We just saw him," I said. "He's on his way. Should Delia and I get into costume?"

"Wait a sec," Les said, motioning with both hands. Then he shouted at the top of his lungs: "Hey, everybody! People! People!"

The set grew silent.

"Before we start this rehearsal," he began, his voice booming through the old house, "I just want to say a few words. Fresh start, everyone. That's what we are doing. Those are my words for today. Fresh start. Let's all put what happened here in the past. Okay? A fresh start. Good. That's all. Energy *up*, everyone! Let's go to work. The bad stuff is behind us."

23

CLAIRE RUINS
A SCENE

IT WAS PRETTY OBVIOUS THAT Les planned to shoot the
kitchen scene. This wasn't just a rehearsal. Why else would
Lazslo be there, and why would the lighting crew have everything in place and the sound guys be scrambling around
the kitchen?

I think Les wanted to take it one step at a time. Make
everyone feel comfortable. Then keep to his shooting
schedule.

I didn't think I could feel comfortable ever again inside
the old house.

When you're like me and you believe that supernatural
and paranormal things can happen, it makes the world a scar-
ier place. Standing in that brightly lit kitchen, I felt super-
alert, like every molecule in my body was tensed and ready
for something weird to happen. Maybe something horrible.

And I couldn't keep Puckerman out of my mind, that furry little man who kept appearing and reappearing where he shouldn't be.

Pulling on my '60s pleated skirt and lacy-collared top beside Delia in the dressing room, I shuddered. Maybe Jake was right. Maybe there *was* a curse on the old house. Maybe . . .

"What's your problem?" Delia's voice cut into my thoughts. "You suddenly turned pale."

"Oh . . . uh . . ." I realized I hadn't told her about seeing Puckerman in the mirrors. But I didn't want her to roll her eyes at me and tell me what a flake I am for seeing strangeness wherever I go.

Also, Delia had a lot on her mind. She was the star of the film now. She had lines to learn and scenes to memorize. She had to be thinking about Lana. She didn't need me freaking her out even more.

"I'm okay," I said. "Just thinking. You know."

When Delia and I returned to the set, we saw Annalee standing with Jeremy behind the kitchen counter. She was snuggling against him, and the two of them were beaming at each other like they were on a Valentine card.

Annalee took a step back as soon as Delia strode into the kitchen. "I was just holding your place," she told Delia. "Till you got back. You know. Like a stand-in."

Delia put on a fake smile. "No problem at all," she said sweetly.

Annalee wants to be the star, I told myself. *Watch out for her.*

Jeremy gazed from Annalee to Delia to me. "Are you three friends?" His dark eyes flashed. A devilish grin spread over his handsome face. "Maybe all three of you would like to come to my place in the Valley, and we could ... uh ... do something."

Annalee giggled.

Before anyone could answer, Les called Jeremy over. A few seconds later, the two of them were screaming at each other.

"You're joking, right?" Les bellowed, gesturing with his clipboard. "You really don't know if you're Randy or Tony?"

Jeremy shrugged. I couldn't hear his answer, but I saw him back away.

"You're standing here and you don't know which part you play? Didn't anyone get you a script?"

"I don't really use a script," Jeremy said. "I usually work in the moment."

Les looked like a grizzly bear ready to pounce. He tossed his clipboard to the floor and balled his hands into fists.

Jeremy's eyes went wide. He backed to the wall. "Look, you only have a five-day commitment for me," he said. "Then I'm off to do a Disney shoot for Bruckheimer. You're wasting precious time, aren't you?"

Les's big chest was heaving up and down. His broad fore-head glistened with sweat. "When you're right, you're right, Jeremy lad. You *are* a waste of time."

Jeremy shut his eyes and wrapped his arms in front of his chest. "I want to see my agent. Is Howie here? Someone get Howie on the phone."

"No need." Les bent down and scooped up his clipboard. He stepped forward and smoothed a hand over Jeremy's shoulder as if brushing something off his shirt. "Let's kiss and make up. It'll be a brief romance, okay? We'll shoot your big death scene, and then you'll be free to go and not read your script for Jerry Bruckheimer."

Jeremy eyed him warily. "We're going to finish up today?"

Les nodded. "First, we have to electrocute you."

Jeremy turned to Delia. "Like in the original movie."

"Like in the original movie," Les repeated. "If you had opened your script, you would see that we're using the same script as the 1960 film. Of course, we've updated it a bit."

Delia whispered in my ear. "Whoa. For a moment, I thought Les was going to *devour* Jeremy."

"Seriously," I whispered back.

I glanced at the silver toaster on the kitchen counter. The image of Randy in the original film being shocked by the toaster flashed back into my mind. Randy surrounded by the crackling, white current. Dancing . . . dancing . . . His arms and legs tossing about, even after he was dead.

I shut my eyes and tried to force the image from my mind. I guessed we were about to see the same scene, this time with Jeremy. I suddenly wondered if Jeremy was a good dancer. The thought made me snicker.

"Okay, everyone. Places," Les shouted. He stood at the kitchen doorway, waving us all up to the counter.

I followed Delia, Annalee, Jeremy, and Aidan, the boy playing Tony, onto the set. I didn't have any lines in this scene. I was just supposed to scream my head off when Jeremy was electrocuted by the toaster.

Becka Tisdale, the script assistant, was having a whispered conversation with Les. She was as tall and needle-thin as Les was squat and chubby, and I always thought they looked like different species whenever they huddled together. She jabbed a finger at the open script in her hand, and Les kept nodding.

Finally, Becka closed her script, turned, and walked out of the kitchen, and Les turned back to us. "Okay. Let's block this out," he said. "For those of you who didn't read your script, you are in a panic, frantic to get out of the house. But to your horror, you find the doors and windows locked. You appear to be trapped. So you—"

"Did we try the basement?" Jeremy interrupted.

"That comes later," Les said. "Unfortunately, you won't be around for that scene. Okay. Let's start here." He rubbed his stubbled cheeks. "You run into the kitchen. Tony, you pick up the phone. You hold it to your ear. You tell everyone it's dead. No dial tone."

Aidan squinted at him. "Dial tone?"

Les groaned. "Old-fashioned phones have a dial tone. You know. A buzzing sound." He pointed at Aidan. "You and Jeremy have an argument. You want to try the upstairs windows. But he says he is starving. He wants to make a sandwich."

"I'm kind of hungry, too," Annalee said. "I only had coffee this morning." She was being cute for Jeremy.

"Please don't interrupt," Les said sharply. "Jeremy starts to search the kitchen for food. You look in the fridge. You pull out drawers and open cabinets. You get more and more frantic, see."

Jeremy snapped his fingers. "Got it, boss."

Les uttered an annoyed sigh, but he continued. "You pull out a loaf of bread. You rip out a few slices. You move to the toaster. Drop the bread into the toaster. Push the lever down. And then you get the shock of your life."

Jeremy nodded. "I have to fake it, right?"

"You have to *act*," Les corrected him. "We don't have any special effects rigged up today. The electrical current will be added in post. So you have to imagine that your body is receiving jolt after jolt of electricity—and you have to make us see it. See it and *feel* it. We want the audience to feel every snap, crackle, and pop."

Jeremy nodded. "I can handle it." He did a crazy dance, bending his knees and flailing his arms above his head, jerking his head forward and back. "Like that, right?"

"Not bad," Les said. "Remember—jolt after jolt. We need to see the rhythm of it. Open your eyes wide. Let your mouth hang slack. Maybe your tongue flops out."

Les turned to the rest of us. "You all scream your guts out. You're so shocked and frightened, you don't do anything to help him. You just stand there and scream."

He swung back to Becka, who stood beside Lazslo in front of the camera. "Did I cover everything?"

She nodded. "I think we're good to go."

"Let's try a run-through," Les said. He stepped away from the door. "Go out and come running in. Breathless. Scared. I want to see it instantly on your faces. Come on. Let's go. Make me proud."

He always said that at every rehearsal. I guess it was supposed to inspire us. You know. Get the adrenaline flowing.

The four of us moved out of the kitchen and waited in the doorway for the PA to slate the scene. "Scene twelve, take one."

Les gave the signal. Then we came running back in, stumbling, pushing one another, our eyes wide, chests heaving up and down, panting and terrified.

The scene was going well until I ruined it.

Aidan and Jeremy argued. Aidan tried to pull Jeremy from the kitchen so we could investigate the upstairs windows. Jeremy tugged free of his grasp and started searching frantically for food.

My eyes went to the toaster. I shouldn't have been looking there, but I couldn't stop myself.

A feeling of cold dread washed over me.

I pictured the boy in the original film, holding the toaster, jerking and dancing inside the crackling current. And then I pictured Lana. Her small white hand sitting by itself on the table.

I stared at the gleaming silver toaster. And I knew what was going to happen to Jeremy. It wasn't just a hunch. It was a powerful flash from the future.

I knew what would happen to him as soon as he pushed the lever.

My breath caught in my throat. My whole body shuddered.

I raised my eyes in time to see Jeremy pull the loaf of bread from the bottom kitchen drawer. He raised it high and pushed it in Aidan's face. "See? Food," he said. "I'm going to make a sandwich. Then we can escape this old house."

He tore two slices of bread from the loaf and tossed the loaf to the counter. Then he turned to the toaster—

—and I leaped forward. I threw myself at the counter, and I shrieked: "No! Don't TOUCH it! Jeremy—don't TOUCH the toaster!"

24

A BAD BURN

"CUT! CUT!" LES SCREAMED.

Then everyone started shouting at once. Les stomped angrily into the kitchen. Becka Tisdale followed him, to help him out, I guess. It took a while to get everyone quiet.

"Claire, what is your problem?" He kind of spit the words at me through gritted teeth, growling like a bear.

"The . . . toaster," I stammered, pointing.

"What about it?"

"I just had a feeling. Like in the old film. I mean . . ." I could barely choke out the words. My pulse was pounding in my ears.

Les angrily grabbed up the toaster in both hands.

"NO!" I screamed.

Les raised the toaster in front of him, showing it off to everyone. "It's not plugged in," he said. "See? No way it can shock Jeremy. Look, Claire. We even cut off the cord." He spun the toaster around. "No cord. No electricity. Okay?"

I lowered my eyes. My hair fell over my face.

Please, kill me now.

"Sorry," I managed to choke out. "I'm really sorry, everyone. I'm . . . totally embarrassed."

Les shook his head. "Let's take a ten-minute break, people, to regroup. Everyone come back refreshed, okay? We're going to film this scene today. Ten minutes. See you back here."

Delia walked over and put her arm around my shoulder. "It's okay," she whispered. "It was only a run-through. What's the big deal?"

Jeremy Dane grinned at me. "Thanks for trying to save my life, Claire," he said. "I didn't know you cared."

"S-sorry," I stammered. I kept my eyes down. I really did feel like a fool. *The toaster wasn't even plugged in.*

"You want to come to my dressing room?" Jeremy said. "We could discuss the scene."

"No thanks," I murmured.

Jeremy nodded and walked away.

I saw Jake standing behind the kitchen counter. I hurried over to him. "Did you see the whole thing? I just changed my image from jerk to total jerk."

"It wasn't that bad," he said. "You didn't ruin a take or anything."

Delia straightened my hair behind my head. "You weren't a total jerk. No way. You had good reason to be afraid. We all saw what happened to Lana."

I picked up the toaster and rolled it around between my hands. The toaster couldn't shock anyone.

Annalee was over by the camera, flirting with one of the crew guys. She saw Jake and flashed him a smile. Les Bachman and Becka were having a discussion, both talking at once.

I set down the toaster. Then I led Jake and Delia to the catering table in the front room, and we grabbed Cokes. "Do you like that guy Jeremy Dane?" Jake asked.

"No way," Delia and I both answered at once.

"He likes himself a lot," Delia said. "He likes to toss his blond hair back and forth like this. He thinks it's a turn-on." She demonstrated. It was pretty funny.

"We don't have to put up with him much longer," I said. "This is his last scene." I brushed a tuft of hair off Jake's forehead. "You have better hair than Jeremy."

"Thanks. It's banging hot out there. You two want to come for a swim when you're finished?"

"Sure," I said. Hey, an actual invitation from Jake. Wow. But he had his eyes on Delia.

"I . . . might be busy," Delia said. Then she added, "Where's Shawn? He doesn't answer my texts."

"Laguna," Jake said. "Dee, you sure you don't want to come over later?"

Before she could answer, Les Bachman interrupted. "Okay, people. It's not getting any earlier. Places, please."

Delia and I set down our Coke cans and hurried back to the set. Annalee patted the crew guy's chest, then trotted into the kitchen. Aidan returned, smelling of cigarette smoke.

"Okay. We've got everyone but our star," Les said.

"Anybody see the great Jeremy? Maybe he decided to read his script." He laughed at his own joke.

"Jeremy Dane? Jeremy?" Becka shouted. Her voice echoed through the big house.

"Probably downstairs in his dressing room," I said. "I'll go get him."

I started toward the back stairway. Delia hurried after me. "I'll go with her," she announced.

The dressing rooms were downstairs in the basement of the old mansion. The steep wooden stairs creaked beneath us as we made our way down, leaning on the narrow banister. "Jeremy! Hey—Jeremy?" I shouted.

No reply.

A row of small dressing rooms began at the bottom of the stairs. The first door was open and yellow light washed out.

I heard rapid footsteps. Running in the other direction.

"Jeremy? Is that you?" I called.

Delia shouted, too. "Hey, Jeremy—you're keeping everyone waiting."

I peered into the open dressing-room door. I saw a mirrored dressing table, a small, open closet, empty, and a table cluttered with food plates and soda cans.

And then I saw Jeremy Dane.

From the back. He appeared to be standing in front of a microwave oven on the wall. He leaned toward the oven, the door open just a crack.

"Jeremy? Hey—Jeremy? What's up?" I called.

Jeremy didn't move.

I grabbed Delia's hand and squeezed it hard as we stepped closer.

And then a groan escaped my throat, and I thought I would toss my breakfast.

Jeremy's head ... his head ... it was *inside the microwave.*

His body stood limp and unmoving, propped against the wall. And his head ...

"He's *burned*!" Delia screamed. "His *whole face* is burned black!"

Yes. I pulled open the microwave door and saw him clearly. His skin was black, like burned meat, and peeling off his face, curling off in flakes.

We both screamed as his body suddenly fell. It collapsed and tumbled heavily to the floor.

I heard a sick *rrrip* sound. And stared in frozen horror ... stared into the oven ... stared ... stared at his melted skin.

Jeremy was crumpled on the floor. But half of his face— half of his face was stuck to the bottom of the microwave.

25

MELTED CHEESE

"WE'VE BEEN MOPING AROUND FOR TWO DAYS," Jake said. "We need to think about something else."

"How *can* we?" I cried. I didn't mean to sound so shrill. "Jake, you didn't see what Delia and I saw. Jeremy's face *melted*. His head was totally black, and his skin was stuck to the microwave. How could that happen? *How?*"

The four of us were in a tiny booth at the Hamburger Hamlet on Larchmont, south of Beverly. It seemed that whenever real horror struck, we had to soothe ourselves with cheeseburgers.

Shawn pulled a long gob of cheese from his burger and lowered it to his mouth.

Delia uttered a groan. "How can you eat *melted cheese* after what we saw?"

I don't know why, but that made me laugh. Yes, Jeremy's face was like melted cheese. But why was I laughing? Nervous laughter, I guess. Laughter to keep from crying.

Shawn shook his head. "The whole thing is impossible. If his head was in the microwave, the door had to be open. And if the door was open, the microwave wouldn't work. I think—"

"Shawn, we've been over this a hundred times," I said. "You're repeating yourself."

"It doesn't make sense—"

"Listen. We saw what we saw. The police said there was an electrical surge, like an explosion. He leaned into the microwave to put in his lunch and . . . it just exploded. He was nuked standing up."

"How can it be an accident?" Delia said softly. She'd only taken one small bite from her cheeseburger. "The police decided it was an accident. But . . . it was just like what happened in the old film." She shivered.

I felt sick. Two days later, and I still felt sick. "His hair was all melted," I said. "It was totally stuck together. Like it had turned to wax. Oh, wow."

Jake pushed his milk shake glass toward me. "Here. Drink some."

My hand shook as I raised the glass to my mouth. I took a sip, then shoved the glass away.

Jake finished his cheeseburger and scooped up the slice of pickle that had fallen onto the plate. I knew what he was trying to do. He was trying to get everyone to act normal.

But how could we?

Delia sighed. "I think some crazy person is trying to re-create the original movie. You know. Kill the people in the mansion one by one the way they were killed in the film."

"That's too sick," Shawn muttered.

"That's way crazy," Jake said. "The police were all over it. They said it was an accident. A horrible accident."

"That's *two* horrible accidents," I muttered. I raised my eyes to Jake. "I'm starting to think you're right. Maybe there *is* a curse on Mayhem Manor."

Delia suddenly uttered a sharp cry and her eyes went wide. "Claire, you're Darlene, right? Does that mean you're *next*?"

Shawn wiped milk shake off his upper lip with the back of his hand. He squinted at me. "I don't believe it. Your parents are going on with the movie?"

I nodded. "Yes. They're desperate to keep it going."

"Our parents hired a ton of security guards," Jake said. "These dudes will be everywhere. I heard my dad say that should make the set safe from now on."

I blinked. "Safe from accidents? How can you be safe from accidents?"

Delia frowned. "Do we each get a security guard? Someone to follow us everywhere we go?"

"Probably," Jake said.

Delia giggled. "I hope mine is cute."

Shawn didn't even bother to ask. He took the cheeseburger from Delia's plate and tilted it to his face.

Jake's phone bleeped. He pulled it from his pocket. I could read it over his shoulder. It was a text from Annalee: *Where r u?*

"We've got to go," he said. He started to slide out of the booth.

Shawn sighed. "A beautiful summer day. Wasted. A day without a wave is a wasted day."

I patted him on the shoulder. "Shawn, you're a poet."

Shawn was right. We stepped out into an amazing L.A. summer day, warm, the air fresh and soft, clear blue skies. The kind of day everyone should be happy. But it was impossible to toss off the gloom.

I couldn't shut the horrifying pictures from my mind. Lana's hand. Jeremy's face. They kept moving through my mind as if they were on a continuous loop. Over and over. I didn't know how to stop them.

We climbed into Jake's Jeep. Without even realizing it, I grabbed his arm. "Do you think you could come over? You know. Stay for a while? I'm feeling kind of . . . shaky."

"Hey, wish I could," he said, "but I'm meeting up with Annalee. I'm kind of late."

I sighed and turned my head to the window.

Jake has satellite radio in his Jeep, and he turned to the blues channel. *My baby left me and I'm feelin' so sad* . . . Perfect.

"Hey, Claire." Delia poked her head into the front. "Get that look off your face. What are you thinking about?"

"Everything," I said. "I'm thinking about everything."

I had no way of knowing that the day held even more horror. And that the horror would come from my dad.

26

HOWLS AND
WHISPERS

IT WAS NOT THE BEST NIGHT to have dinner home alone. But Dad was away. Mom was at some meetings in New York. And Delia's mom was insisting she stay home for some "family time."

So it was just me and Taffy, our black cat, who ignores me and waits under the couch for Mom to return. Cats are boring. And they won't keep you company, even if you beg them.

Maria's sister was sick, so Maria wasn't there to make dinner. Luckily, Mom keeps these frozen burritos in the freezer that aren't bad. I mixed a small salad and nuked a chicken burrito and ate at the kitchen counter with the TV on, a rerun of *Friends*.

My phone rang when I was finishing the last forkful of burrito. I wiped some cheese off my chin and stared at the screen. I didn't recognize the number.

"Hello?"

"Claire, it's Dad. I'm in a little trouble here."

My breath caught in my throat. He didn't sound right. His voice was muffled. "Trouble?"

"Well, yes. I'm at the studio. My car had to be towed. Can you come pick me up?"

"Well . . . sure," I said. "But, Dad—"

"There's no one around to give me a ride. Can you come now?"

"Of course." Why did he sound so weird? "Where will you be, Dad?"

"I'm at Mayhem Manor," he said. "Park the car and come meet me here, okay?"

"Huh? You're at Mayhem Manor? I don't understand."

"I was helping the police. Trying to get them to finish their investigation. I'll be here with them for another half hour. So come meet me here. Just walk through the yellow tape."

"Okay. No problem." I clicked off the phone. I took the last sip of Diet Coke in my glass and went to find the keys to the Volvo.

Why didn't Dad just call a car service?

He sounded really troubled. Maybe the police were giving him a hard time, and he didn't want to wait for a car service. Or maybe he wanted to have some time to talk to me.

All kinds of questions ran through my mind as I drove to Burbank. Did he decide my birthday party at the studio should be canceled? Is that why he wanted to see me?

I scolded myself for being selfish. Dad had a lot more on his mind than my crazy party.

I didn't recognize the night guard in the parking booth. I told him who I was, but he insisted on seeing ID. I didn't see any other cars in the executive lot.

I parked right next to the entrance and hurried through the gate. Most of the buildings were dark, and the streetlamps were dim. A wind came up and howled around the corner of the executive cottages. It was a hot wind, very steamy, and it blew my hair into my face.

I lowered my head and kept walking. In the distance, the twin towers of Mayhem Manor came into view, black against the purple sky. I didn't see any police cars. No signs of life anywhere.

I passed Soundstage A, the high walls casting a black shadow over the ground. An orange light washed out from the commissary windows, but I couldn't see anyone inside.

A ghost town, I thought. Despite the hot wind on my face, a shiver rolled down my back.

I jumped as something scampered across the walk a few feet in front of me. In the dim light, it took a few seconds to see that it was just a paper bag. I scolded myself for being so jumpy. But I'd never been to the studio when it was dark and empty.

And, of course, I had good reason to be jumpy. People had died here, ugly, frightening deaths.

A single light sent a circle of pale silver over the entrance to the old mansion. The house was encircled by yellow police tape. Tape stretched across the front door. The trees on the sides of the house were also wrapped in tape.

But no patrol cars. No cars at all.

Did they leave before I got here? Was Dad still waiting for me inside?

The hot wind howled again, shaking the trees. I heard branches cracking and creaking. I heard the low *hoot hoot* of a night bird nearby. The sound seemed sad and lonely. The bird hooted one more time, then was silent.

I could feel the blood pulsing at my temples. Did I really want to go into Mayhem Manor by myself at night?

Again, I heard Dad's voice on the phone, so strange and muffled. Almost desperate.

I grabbed the yellow tape off the door and tugged it aside. The door stuck. I had to pull hard to make it move. A rush of cold air greeted me as I stepped inside.

Dim lights on the walls sent a shadowy glow over the front hall. I took one cautious step, then another. The floorboards squeaked under my shoes. Ahead of me, the front room stretched in near darkness.

"Dad?" I cupped my hands over my mouth and shouted. "Dad? Are you here?"

I really didn't want to go deeper into the house.

"Hey—Dad?"

Silence. A long howl behind me made my skin creep. I realized I'd left the front door open. The hot wind blew at my back, as if pushing me into the house.

I stepped into the front room. In the darkness, I could

see bookshelves rising up to the high ceilings on three sides. Furniture was clumped in the center of the room, like animals huddled at night. A boom mike tilted against the wall. I could make out a pile of cables and other electronic equipment stacked at the side of the dark fireplace.

"Hey, Dad? It's me. Are you here?"

My voice rang out through the huge house. The wind howled again. The only answer to my calls.

"This is crazy," I murmured. "No way he's still here."

I started to turn back—and saw something move in the shadows of the dining room. Just a flash of movement. A change of the light.

"Dad?"

I took a few steps toward the wide dining-room doorway. "Ohh." I stumbled over something on the floor. Grabbed the back of a leather couch to keep from falling.

Just a cable. A cable stretching to the next room. I struggled to catch my breath.

And heard a whisper.

Not the howl of the gusting wind. Not a sound, but a word. A whispered word: *Claire.*

Yes, I heard my name and froze, still gripping the back of the couch. I froze and listened, my whole body tingling, all my senses alert to every movement and sound.

"*Claaaaaaaiiirrrrre.*"

A hoarse whisper. I suddenly thought of the jacaranda trees in Jake's backyard. That night I heard them whispering my name.

Maybe I imagined that. Maybe I did.

But this was real. Someone was in this old house with me, someone who wanted to frighten me.

"Who's there?" I tried to shout, but my voice came out tiny and weak. "Who is it?"

"Claaaaaire—are you ready?" came the harsh whisper. *"I am almost ready for you, Claire. Are you ready to be a STAR?"*

"Who are you?" I screamed, my voice hollow in the vast, empty room. "Where are you? Is that you, Puckerman? Is that you? Did you bring me here?"

Silence.

A long silence now.

"Wh-who's there?" My voice cracked on the words.

Silence.

The house creaked. I heard the soft shuffle of footsteps. Someone moving quickly. Trying to be silent.

"Who's there?" I screamed. "Who—?"

And someone grabbed me. Two hands roughly gripped my shoulders from behind.

27

A MEAN TRICK

"OHHH." I TRIED TO SCREAM but no sound came out.

I felt myself being spun around. I stared into a blinding circle of white light.

I couldn't see who held me. I struggled to squirm free. "Let . . . go . . ." I whispered.

The hands slid off my shoulders. The bright light swept down to the floor. I gazed at the face in front of me. I saw two eyes beneath a dark cap. A short mustache. A grim expression.

A policeman.

Yes. A policeman with a badge on the shirt pocket of his dark uniform, a flashlight in one hand.

"Sorry to startle you, miss." His voice was soft, just above a whisper. His eyes flashed. "You startled me, too."

"I—I—" I was still trying to catch my breath.

"What are you doing here? This is an investigation scene," he said.

"I . . . you see . . . I came to pick up my father."

He narrowed his eyes at me. "Your father? Your father isn't here. No one is here but me. What's your name?"

"Claire. Claire Woodlawn. My dad is Sy Woodlawn. Was he here with you?"

The cop shook his head. He raised the flashlight to see my face more clearly.

"He called me," I said. "He said to come here."

"Is this a dare?" the cop asked. "Did someone dare you to come here at night? Is that what this is about?"

"No way," I said. "Do you know my dad? He runs this studio. He—"

"Why are you here, Claire? Did you come to do some kind of mischief?"

"Aren't you listening to me?" I screamed. I didn't mean to lose it. But he was refusing to listen. "I came to pick up my father. But then . . . I heard someone . . . someone whispered to me."

"Someone played a joke on you?"

"I don't know. I—"

He raised the light to my face. I had to shield my eyes with my arms.

"Call your father," he said. "Do you have your phone? Call your father, and I'll let you go."

"Okay," I said. My hand was shaking. I reached into my bag. I fumbled around for the phone. "Okay. Okay. I'll call him. He'll tell you."

"Calm down," he said softly. "You don't have to be scared. Just call your father for me."

"Someone whispered things to me," I said. "Someone else is in this house."

"Sometimes old houses make funny noises," he said. He motioned to the phone in my hand. He raised the light to it so I could push my dad's number.

"Put it on speaker," he said.

My dad answered after three rings. "Hello? Claire?"

"Dad, I came to the studio to pick you up, but—"

"You did *what*? Where *are* you?"

"At the studio. I—"

"Claire, I texted you this morning, remember? I'm in Chicago. At the media convention. Didn't you see my text?"

"You're in Chicago?"

"Yes. I'll be home on Monday. I can't really talk. In the middle of a meeting thing. Everything okay?"

"Yeah. I guess."

He clicked off.

I raised my eyes to the police officer. He had a smile on his face, for some reason. "Claire, someone played a mean trick on you. Show me your driver's license and you can go home."

I couldn't go back to that empty house. I felt shaky and tense, like all my muscles had tightened up and my heart was clogging my throat.

Someone wanted to frighten me. Someone tricked me into the old mansion.

He whispered my name. He whispered things to scare me.

What would he have done if that cop hadn't been there?

I pulled my car up Jake's driveway. I needed Jake to be nice to me. Tonight I knew Jake could make the difference.

Crazy thoughts.

I could see Mrs. Castellano in the kitchen window. I banged on the door, and she pulled it open.

"How are you, dear?"

"Okay," I said. "Is Jake—?"

"He went to a movie," she said. "With Annalee Franklin, I think. He told me the movie but I forget it."

"That's okay," I said. "It wasn't important." I pictured Annalee all over Jake in the back of a movie theater. It didn't improve my mood. Actually, I had to force myself not to burst out crying in front of his mom.

"If . . . if he gets home early, tell him I'd like to see him," I stammered. Then I said good night and climbed back in the car. *I'm messed up. Too emotional to live.*

Back home, I turned on every light in the house. Then I called Delia. "Come over. Don't say a word. Just come over. Hurry."

Delia arrived fifteen minutes later. "Thanks for rescuing me, Claire." She hugged me. "Bad night at my house. I was glad to get out."

"Why? What's up?"

"You know. My mom's boyfriend. It's always about him. He was grooming some huge dog, some kind of weird shepherd, and it bit him. Oh, wow. End-of-the-world time. It was a tiny scratch, but he started screaming about rabies, and I burst out laughing, so he and Mom got in *my* face. Like I'm the one who bit him. He's a total baby. I mean, he grooms dogs, right? So what does he expect? That they're *not* going to bite him?"

I laughed. Delia could always make me laugh.

"If I was a dog, I'd bite him," Delia said. "Only he'd probably give me rabies. Anyway, I can't stay over. My mom said I had to be back."

She noticed me standing there with my arms wrapped around my chest. "How was your night, Claire?"

"Not great," I said. We walked into the den, each sprawled on a couch, and I told her the whole frightening story.

When I finished, she sat there, picking at the leather couch arm with her long purple nails, her mouth hanging open. "Who do you think it was? Do you think it's the little hairy guy from the trailer with the potions?"

"Maybe. I don't know. There was a policeman there. I tried to tell him someone else was in the old house. I don't think he believed me at all." I raked my hair back from my face with one hand. "I don't know what to do. Really."

"Did you tell your dad?"

"I couldn't. He's in Chicago. In a meeting."

"Maybe you should quit the movie, Claire. I mean—"

"How can I? I'm already in several scenes. They'd have to start shooting from the beginning. Besides, how many years have I been waiting for this chance?"

She narrowed her eyes at me. "The chance to be *killed*?"

There wasn't much to say after that.

We tried talking about other things, but it was just awkward. Normally, we could make jokes about what had happened. But this was too scary to be funny.

When we heard a loud pounding on the kitchen door, we both jumped to our feet with startled cries.

Delia and I walked to the kitchen together. We stopped in the doorway and peered through the window of the back door. Jake peered back at us.

I pulled open the door, and he stepped in. His hair was wild and unbrushed. He wore khaki cargo shorts and a maroon-and-gold Beverly Hills Academy tennis team jersey.

"Hey, what's up?" He had his eyes on Delia.

"I saw your mom," I said. "I told her—"

He grinned. "You two want to get something to eat?"

"No," I said sharply. "I . . . I had a scary night, and I needed someone to talk to and—"

"I'm late," Delia said, gazing at her phone. "Got to get back to the dog pound."

"You want me to go with you or something?" Jake asked her.

She rolled her eyes. "No thanks. Listen, Claire, lock the doors, okay? Talk to you in the morning." She hurried out.

Jake turned to me. "What was *that* about?"

"I'll tell you," I said. I motioned for him to sit at the kitchen counter. "I had a scary night. I—"

He dropped onto one of the tall stools, and I took the one beside him. "Hey, Claire, did you talk to Delia?"

"Talk to Delia?"

"You know," he said. "Did you ever tell Delia I'm kind of hot for her?"

I raised my hands to strangle him. That was the last straw. If I killed him now, it would be justifiable homicide.

But I suddenly had a better idea.

I scooted off the kitchen stool. "Jake, I'll be right back. Don't move, okay?"

He folded his arms on the counter and rested his head on them. "Where are you going?"

"Just don't move. I'll be back in a sec."

I knew what I had to do. I needed to set things right with Jake right now. Annalee . . . Delia . . . He was hot for both of them. And me? I was some kind of insect species he didn't even see.

I'd been very patient. But enough was enough. I couldn't take it anymore.

And I didn't have to. I had the potion. The love potion I'd grabbed from that creep Puckerman's trailer. And the time had come to use it.

28

THE POTION
WORKS

UPSTAIRS IN MY BEDROOM, I fumbled around in my bag until my fingers wrapped around the little potion bottle. I pulled it out and squinted at the gray powder inside.

A few flakes. That's all it would take, and the whole confusion, the whole waiting for Jake to notice me would be over.

As I gazed at the little bottle, I believed. I totally believed it would work.

I jogged back to the kitchen. Yes, my heart was flipping and flopping in my chest. But it wasn't fear. It wasn't anxiety. It was excitement.

I stepped into the bright lights of the kitchen. Jake still had his head down on the counter. I crept up behind him and carefully twisted off the cap to the bottle.

He started to raise his head.

"Don't turn around till I tell you," I said. "I have a surprise."

He snickered. "A surprise?"

"Don't turn around," I repeated. I dipped my thumb and finger into the gray powder. Then I raised my hand over the back of his head and dropped a few tiny flakes onto his hair.

There's no one else here. I'll be the first one he sees. And he'll be desperately in love with me. Finally.

I closed the bottle and tucked it into my jeans pocket. "Okay," I said, "raise your head."

He obediently sat up straight. I scooted around the counter and stood in front of him. He stared at me, his face wrinkling in confusion. "Where's the surprise, Claire?"

I gave him a teasing smile. "Feel strange or anything?"

He blinked. "Strange? No. Why? What's up?"

"Just wait," I said, patting his hand. "Wait. Keep watching me and wait."

"I don't get it," he said.

I couldn't hold it in. "I just gave you a love potion, Jake," I said. Then I dove forward and kissed him. I placed my hands behind his head and pressed my lips hard against his lips. I waited for him to kiss me back.

But something was wrong.

His lips felt so dry. Like wrinkled paper.

"Ohh." I jumped back to see what was wrong. And I uttered a moan of horror as he started to change.

His papery lips flaked off like dandruff. Then the color of his eyes faded to gray. The skin on his face . . . it sagged. It appeared to grow loose, flabby—and a white stubble formed on his cheeks and chin.

"Oh no. Oh my god," I moaned. My excitement quickly turned to horror as I watched Jake's hair fall out in clumps. His forehead appeared to bulge as the hair fell to the counter. The skin on his forehead became pale and scaly. In seconds, he was totally bald except for a fringe of white hair around his ears.

His body slumped over the counter. He seemed to grow smaller. Like he was disappearing into his shirt, which hung loose around him.

It took less than a minute. I hadn't moved the whole time. I could still feel the taste of his powdery lips on mine. I stood there with my hands pressed to my cheeks, watching . . . watching without breathing.

Watching Jake turn into an old man.

Yes. I stared at an old Jake. At least eighty or ninety years old.

He blinked his eyes and coughed. His gray eyes were watery. The skin on his bald head was peeling. He clicked his teeth a few times. Then he glanced at the kitchen clock over my shoulder. "Past my bedtime," he croaked in a hoarse, old man's voice. "How'd it get to be so late?"

29

DARLENE DIES AGAIN

"DEE, YOU'VE GOT TO COME BACK. I . . . I don't know what to do."

"I can't, Claire. I just pulled into my driveway. Mom is watching me from the window."

"But I need help. Don't you understand? I stole the wrong potion from Puckerman's trailer. Again."

"Another *hate* potion? You didn't! What's Jake doing? Is he threatening you?"

"No. No. You don't understand. It must be an *aging* potion. He's like sitting there half asleep. He keeps clicking his teeth and making horrible breathing noises. Like he has asthma or something. He . . . he looks horrible, Dee. He's ancient. I mean, I made him totally *old*."

"Claire, you're screaming. Take a breath."

"He just rubbed his face with his hands. His hands are all wrinkled and they have ugly brown spots all over the backs. He's totally bald, Dee. What can I do? Who can I call? Do you think he's going to *die*?"

"Why? Is he sick? Just because he's old doesn't mean—"

"I could go to prison for this, right? How will I tell his parents? What can I say? I—I . . . can't think straight. I need help."

"Okay, okay. I'm backing down the driveway. I'm coming back. But I don't see what I can do to help. I mean—"

"Oh, wait. Delia. Wait. Something's happening to him."

"Is he dying?"

"No. I don't know. He's sort of squirming on the kitchen stool. He keeps blinking. Oh my god. Oh my god. Have I killed him? Have I killed Jake? What's happening to him?"

"Try to stay calm, Claire. You're totally freaking me out, and I can't even see him. Hey—I just went through a stop sign. Oh, wow. It's past the curfew, right? I'm not supposed to be driving."

"He . . . he's changing again, Delia. His face—it's like tightening up. I'm staring at his hands. The brown spots faded away. He . . . he sat up straight. I don't believe it. His hair is growing back. It's like one of those reverse movies. He's growing young. Really. He—"

"It wore off? The potion wore off? Just like when we gave him and Shawn that *hate* potion?"

"Yes. I think so. His eyes are blue again. He's staring hard at me. I wonder if he'll remember . . . if he realizes . . . I'm getting off, Dee. You'd better go home. I think it's okay here. I'll talk to you in the morning."

Jake gripped the edge of the counter as if trying to keep

his balance. He was back to himself. At least, he looked like himself. His hair was just as thick and unruly as before, his eyes the old clear blue, his face young, hands unwrinkled.

He blinked a few more times. Then he turned to me. "Hey, Claire, you have anything to eat? I'm suddenly like totally starving."

The next day, Delia and I watched the last part of the original *Mayhem Manor* movie again.

I know it's crazy. But everything happening was making us crazy. Wouldn't *you* be a little insane?

The studio was still closed down while the police investigated the two accidents. Jake was back to himself and didn't remember a thing about last night. He and Shawn were at the beach, in Santa Monica, I think. Mom was in New York. Dad was in Chicago. Taffy was under the couch.

Normal life, if you live my life. But I didn't feel like it was normal. I felt like something really terrifying was going on here, and maybe the most terrifying part was still to come.

Just one of my crazy hunches? Maybe. But for once, Delia agreed with me. And so we decided to watch some of the old film again, just to see if maybe there was a clue there. Something we missed. Something that might help us get through this film shoot alive.

We both grabbed bottles of coconut water from the fridge and made our way downstairs to my family's screening room. Dad had been watching rushes from *Please Don't,* the comedy the studio was producing. I found the *Mayhem Manor* DVD under a stack of new movie disks.

I slid it into the player, adjusted the volume, then skipped past the Cindy and Randy dying scenes. I wanted to watch Darlene die again. After all, I was Darlene.

I dropped down beside Dee in the front row of seats. I wanted to watch Darlene's scene—and I *didn't* want to watch it. I had this heavy feeling of dread I'd never known before, like a two-ton weight pressing me down. It isn't easy to watch someone actually dying.

The black-and-white images reflected off the screen, their shadows dancing over the two of us. It made me feel like I was part of the old film.

I took a long gulp of the sweet water. I hadn't felt hungry for days. But now I felt empty, like something was gnawing at my stomach.

"Only four kids left," Delia said. "Sue, Tony, Brian, and Darlene." She took a long drink from the water bottle. "This is why I hate horror movies. There's too much horror."

For some reason, that made us both burst out laughing.

When the scene began, the teens were frantic. Darlene was crying. She knelt down beside Randy and held him by the shoulders. He was sprawled dead on the floor. His skin was burned black.

Tony banged his fists on the wall angrily. Brian stared wide-eyed as if he'd gone into a trance. "We've got to get it together," Tony said. "We've got to think, think . . ."

"We've got to get out of this house before . . . before

someone kills us all," Brian said, sounding as if he had trouble remembering his lines.

Darlene set Randy's charred head down. Then she climbed to her feet. "Brian is right. Let's go. Let's just get out."

"Who is doing this to us?" Brian cried, pressing his hands to the sides of his face. "What crazy maniac wants to kill us all?"

Tony shook his head at Brian. "Get it together, man. If you lose your cool now, you'll never get out of here."

"Upstairs," Darlene said. "Maybe we can climb out an upstairs window."

"Oh, wow," Delia murmured. "Don't do it, Darlene. Don't run up those stairs."

I could feel all my muscles tense. I had seen this scene before. But, of course, I didn't know then that I'd be the one running up the steps.

The four teens stood at the bottom of the steep stairway. They gazed up into the darkness at the top. They hesitated.

"Are you sure you want to go up there?" Brian asked. "It's so dark, man."

"We have no choice," Darlene said, pushing the two boys aside, "if we want to get out of this house alive." She raised her foot to the first step. "Follow me."

"Don't do it! Don't *do* it!" Delia screamed at the screen.

But we watched Darlene go running up the creaky old steps.

I gasped as she fell. The camera angle went higher, and

once again I saw there was no step there. The top boards were missing. It was an open hole.

Darlene screamed as her whole body dropped into the hole. She fell quickly. She raised her arms to stop herself, but she wasn't quick enough. Her shrill scream was cut off by a sickening *craaack*.

The sound of her neck breaking.

"Turn it off! STOP it!" Delia cried, covering her face. "STOP it!"

"No. Wait," I said. "Look. Delia, look." I shook her. I forced her to open her eyes.

And we both stared at the little man who appeared briefly at the end of Darlene's death scene. The bearded, hairy little man who suddenly popped onto the set.

"It's him!" I screamed. "Puckerman."

Delia squinted at the screen. "The little fur ball?"

"Yes," I cried. "Yes. But how can that be? That was sixty years ago! And look at him. He looks exactly the same."

The screen went blank.

"I've never seen him," Delia said. "You're the only one who's seen him. Are you sure it's the same dude? It *can't* be—can it?"

"It is," I murmured. "It's him."

"But—how? How could the same weird little guy be there? What was he *doing* there?"

"I don't know," I said, feeling a chill roll down my back. "But I'm going to find out."

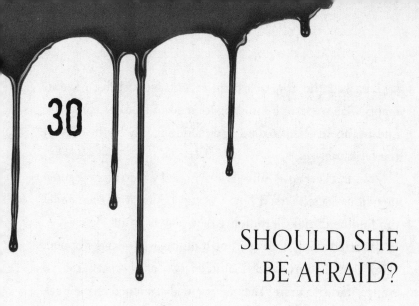

30

SHOULD SHE BE AFRAID?

THE STUDIO WAS REOPENED THE next morning. I got a call to be on the set at nine.

I drove there early because I had a mission to accomplish before I returned to Mayhem Manor. My plan was to confront Benny Puckerman, to insist he answer my questions. I planned to stay in his face until he explained everything.

It was a horror-movie-type day. Dark with low storm clouds rolling rapidly overhead. Swirling winds pushed my car from side to side as I inched through rush-hour traffic to Burbank.

Three patrol cars were parked outside the executive lot. The police investigation was continuing. I found a parking space in the back, worked up my courage, and, ducking under a few scattered raindrops, started toward Puckerman's trailer.

I passed the row of executive cottages, still dark and empty. The wardrobe building loomed in front of me at the end of the street. I turned and made my way to the side of the building.

"Mr. Puckerman—uh—Puck? I need you to answer some questions." I rehearsed how I would begin. My voice came out high and shaky. I didn't realize how nervous I felt.

I started along the wardrobe building wall—and stopped. "Oh, wow," I murmured. I blinked two or three times. No trailer. It wasn't there. The narrow road stretched to the back of the building and ended with a dark fence.

"Perfect," I muttered. "He's gone." Had he moved his trailer to another part of the studio?

I turned and started toward the commissary. I was so early I had time for a cup of coffee. Wiping a raindrop off my forehead, I saw Betty Hecht hunched at the front door of the wardrobe building. Her red hair was tucked into the hood of a yellow rain slicker. She was struggling with the key to the door.

She called out when she saw me walk by. "Claire? Need an umbrella? I think it's going to pour."

"I'm okay," I said. I took a few steps toward her. "You're here early."

She got the key to work and pushed open the door. "Yes. I got an early call. Lots of wardrobe changes at *Please Don't* today." She sighed. "Everyone's eager to get back to work after . . . after all the trouble."

"Me, too," I said. "Can I ask you a question?" I pointed.

"The trailer at the side of the building? Did they move it?"

She pulled back the slicker hood and shook out her hair. "Trailer?"

"Yeah," I said. "The one that was right back there?"

"There's no trailer over there," she said. "What kind of trailer?"

"There was a man inside it and all kinds of jars and bottles. A short little man with a black beard and bushy black hair."

She made a face, thinking hard. "Claire, do you think we should call security? You saw a suspicious man behind this building?"

"He said his name was Puckerman," I said.

She frowned. "Sounds like a made-up name. I'd better call the studio guards right away. We have to report anything we see after these horrible deaths."

"I . . . I don't think he was dangerous," I said. "I mean, he was sitting in the trailer. Like he belonged there."

"But there *is* no trailer," she insisted.

I decided not to tell Betty about the magic potions. She would probably think I was making some kind of joke, pulling a prank.

"I'll tell my dad about it," I said. "Take care, Betty. I'd better get to the set."

"I'll keep my eyes open," she called as I hurried away. "Can't be too careful these days."

The morning rehearsal went okay, although it was hard to get used to the gray-uniformed security guys crawling everywhere like ants. We all knew why they were there, but it was still creepy to have these tough-looking dudes watching our every move. And they all had revolvers in holsters at their waists.

Was I tense much? Three guesses. I knew the stairway scene was coming up tomorrow, and I had to convince myself over and over that I wasn't going to die the way Darlene in the old movie died.

Delia seemed more worried than anyone. "I promise I'll make sure they double-check every stair," she said. "No way there will be a hole for you to fall in."

The rehearsal ended at noon. Les Bachman had afternoon meetings, so he sent us home early.

That night after dinner, I was on my way to my room to text Jake and see if he wanted to hang out. And I wanted to make sure he hadn't turned back into a ninety-year-old again. I knew I'd have nightmares about that forever.

But Dad stopped me in the hall. "Claire, do you have a minute to talk?"

"Sure," I said. "What's up? You—you don't look good."

Dad sighed. He definitely looked a lot older. "Guess you might say I'm a little stressed. We can't have any more accidents on that set. The police . . . the endless investigation . . .

I don't want the studio to be known forever just as a death scene."

He rubbed his eyes. "I'll be honest with you. After all the trouble, we probably should stop this production. But if we do, the studio will fold. It's do or die for us. We're under a lot of pressure, Claire."

He guided me into the den. He motioned for me to sit in the black leather armchair. Then he dropped wearily into the armchair beside me. He sighed again. "Maybe we should just call it a day. I don't know. The Castellanos want to shut it down. We know we're facing lawsuits from Lana and from Jeremy Dane's people. It's going to be expensive."

"Sorry," I murmured. I didn't really know what to say. I pictured Jeremy's melted head.

"It's impossible to run an old-fashioned kind of studio these days," Dad said, frowning. "It's taken everything we have to keep things going. If we can finish this film without any more horrible incidents . . ." His voice trailed off.

Finally, he raised his gaze to me. "I know acting in this film has meant a lot to you. But—"

"You know, *my* big death scene is coming up next." I don't know why I blurted that out. I guess it was just on my mind.

He squeezed my hand. "I'll make sure you're okay. You'll have more security than the president."

I pushed back against the soft leather. I tapped one hand against the chair arm. "Have you heard from Mom?"

He nodded. "She's still in New York. Her meetings are going pretty well, I guess. She'll be there till Saturday. Then she'll come home a limp noodle. Exhausted. You know how she is after these trips."

"She hates flying so much. She told me she takes enough Ambien to put her out for the whole flight. She's so funny. All her hilarious expressions. She told me she sleeps like a bird."

Dad chuckled. He pulled out his phone and squinted at it. Then he tucked it back in his pocket.

"Don't worry about your birthday party," he said. "None of this will affect your party. We're still going all out. It really will be A Midsummer Night's Dream. We'll light up the trees. Have bands playing everywhere. A dance floor. People walking around in fabulous costumes. Like a dream."

"Awesome," I said. A little bit of the gloom seemed to lift off him as he described the party plans.

"We'll open the whole studio. Let everyone go wherever they please. We'll have a band in the plaza by the front gate. And a band in front of the commissary. You can choose the bands. Maybe we'll open Soundstage B and let kids film whatever they want. You know. Birthday greetings or whatever."

"Excellent. I really can't wait, Dad. I've been thinking about my party nonstop."

He raised tired eyes to me. "It will be good for the studio, too. A huge party will bring a lot of press and media attention. And it'll remind people that the studio can be a magical place. Not a place for crime scene investigations and horrible deaths."

"That's true, and—"

"We'll close off Mayhem Manor. We'll leave the whole back lot dark. Your guests won't have to go anywhere near it. In fact, we'll put up security and make sure no one goes near."

"Brilliant," I said. I leaned forward and kissed his forehead. "You're the best."

His phone buzzed. "Have to take this call."

I jumped up and ran to my room to call Delia. I had to tell her about the party plans. She picked up on the third ring. I heard music in the background. "Where are you?"

"I'm on Sunset," she said. "Just driving around."

"Huh? By yourself? Why didn't you invite me to go with you?"

A pause. "I don't know. Just felt like being alone, I guess."

"Delia, you're still upset about me doing the stairway scene tomorrow?"

"You mean you're *not*?"

"Nothing's going to happen."

Silence.

"I was just about to text Jake. See if he wants to hang out," I said.

"Don't waste a text," she replied.

"What do you mean?"

"Before I left home, I checked Annalee's Facebook page. Don't go there. Unless you want to see a lot of photos of Jake on a couch with Annalee, and the two of them lip-locked in every shot. It looks like they're trying to eat each other's face."

I groaned. "Annalee strikes again. Is there any boy she hasn't had?"

Delia replied, but the phone cut out for a second.

After the disaster with the potion last night, I'd decided to finally tell Jake plain and simple how I feel about him. But now, he'd probably just laugh in my face. Or maybe run away. Whatever I said, it would be *awk-ward*.

I lose.

I lose and Annalee wins.

I suddenly felt like I could cry. Instead, I said, "Delia, I'll be okay tomorrow. Really."

"Tell that to Jeremy."

"Shut up. I mean it. Shut up. There are security dudes every inch of the studio. And those stairs will be totally checked. I'll be fine. I know it."

But as I changed the subject and started to tell her about my birthday party, my sadness about Jake was replaced with a heavy feeling in the pit of my stomach. A heavy feeling of dread.

What if Delia was right? What if everything *wasn't* going to be fine?

31

"THOSE STAIRS LOOK NASTY"

THE NEXT MORNING, DAD DROVE Delia and me to the studio. The sun was finally out, the winds had stopped, and it was a beautiful L.A. summer day.

But it was nearly silent in the car. Dad was thinking hard about something and kept his eyes on the road. In the backseat, Delia kept her hands clasped tightly together as if she were praying. I fiddled with the satellite radio, moving between the pop stations.

Dad always pretended to like the new music. But I could see that Ke$ha was annoying him. I clicked off the radio. "Dad, what are you thinking about?"

He smiled. "Actually, I'm thinking about *A Midsummer Night's Dream*. Aren't there a lot of fairies in that play? Fairies that play tricks on humans in the woods?"

"That's the one," Delia chimed in from the backseat. "We

read it last year. It was supposed to be a comedy, but it wasn't very funny."

"We did a college production at USC," Dad said. "I tried out for Puck, I remember. But I didn't get it. I—"

"Whoa!" Delia and I both cried out.

"What did you say?" I demanded.

"I tried out for Puck. And—"

"Puck!" I cried. "Oh my god!" I turned back to Delia. She looked as excited and surprised as I was.

"Are we dumb or what? Why didn't we remember?" I said. "Puck. Of course. From the play. How could we forget that name?"

Dad started talking about the USC production he was in, telling us some funny things that happened. But I didn't listen. I was thinking about the Puck in the Shakespeare play, trying to remember what he does.

I was still thinking about it when we arrived at the studio. We said good-bye to Dad and made our way to Mayhem Manor. The studio was crowded and busy today. I think they were filming a big musical production number for *Please Don't*.

Two security guards stood beside the makeup trailer. One of them nodded and said good morning as Delia and I entered. The other one studied us with eyes narrowed to slits and didn't speak.

Another security guy, whose big belly poked out of his tight gray uniform shirt, watched us enter the dressing room. We pulled on our '60s outfits. I adjusted the tight straight skirt.

We studied ourselves in the full-length wall mirror. Our clothes had to match the last day's shooting exactly.

Delia didn't speak. "Are you okay?" I asked.

She sniffed. "I don't think so. I'm scared for you. Really."

I shook my head. "Everything bad has already happened. It's over. Think positive."

She rolled her eyes. "You never change. Big smile in a thunderstorm."

I laughed. "That sounds like one of my mom's sayings."

At the entrance to the old mansion, a lanky, red-haired security guard asked our names and checked us off on his clipboard. Inside, we were greeted by the usual cold, damp air. Voices echoed off the high walls, and we heard the rumble of equipment being moved around.

I hesitated. Delia took my arm and led me onto the set. Les Bachman was doing his angry number, arguing with a crew member, tossing his hands in the air and pacing back and forth in front of the guy.

"Look. There's Annalee." Delia pointed.

I heard Annalee's teasing laugh. Then I saw her near the far wall in deep shadow. Who was standing behind her? I squinted to see.

It was Jake, and he had his arms around her from behind. He was holding her close to him. She turned her head and they kissed.

I had a sinking feeling. Like my whole body suddenly weighed two tons and I was about to drop to the floor. I turned away. My chest felt all fluttery.

"Seriously. Doesn't Annalee ever quit?" Delia said, rolling her eyes.

I felt too upset to answer her.

I realized I still had the aging potion in my bag.

I could turn Annalee into a ninety-year-old woman.

The thought cheered me up a little.

I glanced around. I saw more guards standing tensely near the set. Dad wasn't kidding around. He really didn't want any more horrible incidents.

Les came running over to greet us. "Hope you have your running shoes on, kiddo."

"I'm . . . a little nervous," I stammered.

"That's good," Les said. "Get the adrenaline going. Don't worry. We'll do a couple of run-throughs. You know the drill."

I nodded. "Darlene is desperate to get out of the house. I lead the way up the stairs. I run all the way up, looking terrified. The others follow me."

"Good." Les brushed a lint ball off the shoulder of my blouse. "In the original movie, your character fell through a hole in the stairs. But we're not going to do that. We have much more horrifying things planned for you all in the rooms upstairs."

That made me smile. "Awesome. I really don't want to fall through any stairs."

Les rubbed his stubbled jaw. "You wouldn't have to do the fall anyway. We'd use a stunt person." He snickered. "Can't have you risking any broken bones, can we?"

He took out a soiled handkerchief and blew his nose. "The dust in here is killing me. I may sue your parents. Really."

Before I could say anything, he spun away and strode back to the man he'd been arguing with. Shouting and gesturing, he picked up the argument where it had left off.

I turned to Delia. I felt a little more like myself. Les really did make me feel better about the scene.

We walked over to the catering table and had some papaya juice. I devoured a cranberry muffin. I was suddenly starving for some reason. Delia, the Cupcake Queen, said she didn't have any appetite at all.

Actually, she's a good friend, I thought. *Someone who would pass up a muffin because she's worried about me.*

When Les called everyone to the set, I felt the tension sweep over me again. My stomach felt heavy. I wished I hadn't had that muffin.

"Come on, people!" he shouted. "You're not getting paid to loiter. That's *my* job."

We all followed Les to the front stairway. The stairs were carpeted, but the carpet was torn and stained, and the dark wood on some steps showed through ragged holes.

My throat tightened, and I suddenly felt dizzy as the stairway scene in the original film played through my mind. And once again, I saw Darlene drop into the open step. I saw her body slide down till her head caught on the stair frame.

And heard the *crack* of her neck as it broke, killing her instantly.

Wow.

Killing her for real. That poor actress. What a hideous death she had.

Two crew members in baggy jeans and sleeveless t-shirts were halfway up the stairs, on their hands and knees, working to staple microphone cords in place. I guessed Les wanted to get the *thud* of the shoes as we ran up to the second floor.

Annalee stepped up beside Delia and me. She flashed me a smile. I recognized it. It was a victory smile. *I win and you lose, Claire.*

"Do you two have any lines?" she asked. "I don't say anything. I just run up the stairs after Brian and Tony and you two."

"It's just a running scene," I said. "I think we're too scared to say anything. We just want to get upstairs."

She nodded. "Well, don't trip. Those stairs look nasty."

Good advice. What would we do without her?

I turned and watched as the two crew guys finished up and came lumbering down the stairs. One of them stopped and said something to Les. Then he followed his partner to the side.

Les turned to us. "Okay. A run-through. Sorry to keep everyone waiting. You know the drill. You're terrified. You're desperate to get upstairs. Claire leads the way."

He scratched his head. Gave his clipboard a quick glance.

Then motioned to me. "You ready? Okay. Look frightened. Good. That's good. Now run."

I took a deep breath, locked a terrified expression on my face—and started toward the stairs.

32

ANOTHER DEATH
IN THE HOUSE

LES BACHMAN STOPPED ME BEFORE I reached the steps. I was breathing hard, my shoulders heaving up and down, even though I hadn't started to run.

"Whoa. Hold up," he said. "Before we do this run-through, maybe I should explain it better." He took my chin in his hand and tilted my head up toward the top of the stairway. "See? Up there?"

"Huh?" I stared up the stairs. What was Les showing me?

"That's a camera up there," Les said, finally letting go of my chin. "We're filming from the top and the side of the stairs. So, Claire, dear, as you run, don't look up. Don't look at the camera."

"But if I'm running up the stairs, I *have* to look up," I insisted. "Don't you look where you're going when you go up stairs?"

"Just don't look at the camera," Les said. "Dart your eyes from side to side. You're terrified, remember? And look behind you as you climb. You want to see what your friends are doing."

I nodded. "Got it."

"Same goes for the rest of you," Les barked, turning to the two boys, Delia, and Annalee. "You four follow Claire. So keep your eyes on her. If you look in the camera, no one will believe you're afraid. They'll all think you're in on the joke. Know what I'm saying?"

We all muttered yes.

"Can I ask a question?" My voice came out tiny and high.

Les nodded. "Shoot."

I hesitated. "You told me before, but just tell me again." I pointed toward the top. "The stair doesn't give in, right? I don't fall into an open step?"

Les shook his head from side to side. "Claire, Claire, Claire." He chuckled. "I told you this ten minutes ago. Why are you so frightened? Would I allow one of my stars to fall into an open step? Of course I wouldn't."

I was breathing hard. I couldn't help it. I felt right on the edge of total panic. No way to fight it back.

"Sorry," I said to Les. "I saw the original film, and—"

"Here. Watch me," Les said. He handed his clipboard to an assistant. "I'll climb the stairs. I'll show you they are perfectly safe. Sorry you don't trust me." He grumbled some words under his breath.

"No. I do. I *do*," I protested. I stepped in front of the

stairway to block his path. "You don't have to climb the stairs. I can do it. I'm sorry. I mean, sorry for holding everyone up. Let's do it."

Les nodded. He took back his clipboard. "Places, everyone. Get your expressions on. You're terrified, remember. You've got to show it as you follow Claire up the stairs."

He groaned. "Come on, people. This is the *easy* shot. Wait till you see what I have planned for you upstairs in the *next* scene."

I tensed my muscles. I struggled to stop trembling. My stomach rumbled.

I knew I was being crazy. The whole shot would take less than thirty seconds. Look scared. Run to the top. Don't look in the camera.

Easy as banana cream pie, as my mom would say.

I turned and flashed Delia a thumbs-up.

She nodded and forced a smile. Beside her, Annalee pulled down the front of her shift so her boobs would show more. She ran her hands back through her silky black hair, then shook her hair out.

"Okay. Action," Les said, backing away.

I tensed my arms at my sides. I balled my hands into tight fists. I took a few steps toward the stairway, then stopped.

I tried to hold them back. But when I turned to Les, tears filled my eyes. "I'm sorry," I uttered. "I'm having so much trouble here." I motioned toward the stairs. "I just have such a bad feeling."

Suddenly, I saw Annalee brush past Delia. She trotted

over to me, then moved toward the steps. "Watch me, Claire," she said. "I'll do it for you. Look. There's nothing to it."

"Annalee—" Les called.

"No. Wait—" I called.

But she wanted to show everyone how much better she was than me. She was already on the stairs. Already running full speed, one hand sliding up the slender banister. Her straight black hair bobbed behind her. Her shoes thudded the wooden steps hard.

She reached the top in a few seconds. Then she turned and gestured to me with a pleased smile. "See? Easy."

She started down. One step. Two steps. Then she appeared to stumble.

Her hands flew up. Her mouth opened in a scream, a *terrifying*, shrill animal scream. I know I'll hear it forever.

Annalee dropped fast.

The top of the step—it cracked and splintered. And she fell into it. Fell into the open step and dropped, screaming. Screaming a horrible animal wail.

The scream ended with a sick *craaack*. The sound of her neck snapping.

Frozen in horror, I stared up at Annalee's head.

Only her head was visible now, caught on the stair edge. Her head with its green eyes bulging open. Her head. Only her head.

Her mouth, still wide open for its final scream, closed slowly. And then her head sank out of sight.

I covered my eyes with both hands and, my whole body shaking violently, I sank to my knees.

33

FINISH THE FILM?

DELIA AND I KNEW THAT CUPCAKES wouldn't help this time. So we drove to The Cheesecake Factory on Beverly and ordered humongous wedges of chocolate-chip cheesecake piled high with whipped cream.

Whenever tragedy struck, we sank into a deep depression for days. Then how did we pull ourselves out of it? We went out to eat something sinful.

Okay. I know it's lame. Tell me about it. But come on. Haven't you ever wanted to drown your sorrows in cheesecake?

If only we had boyfriends. I know, that's not the answer to anything. But, wow, they could have distracted us from our dreary thoughts.

All week, Jake acted totally wrecked by Annalee's death. Maybe he really cared about her. But the way he kept trying to get Delia to comfort him made me wonder.

I tried to get his attention. I went over to his house to have a serious talk with him. But Shawn was there, getting in my face, being annoying.

Finally, I snapped at him, "Shawn, what do you *want*?"

He flashed me a toothy grin. "I want to rock your world."

Oh, gross.

Why can't guys take a hint and get lost when you want them to?

As for Jake, I was ready to give up. The whole situation made me think of one of my mom's weird expressions: "You're barking up a brick wall." And that's what I was doing with Jake. Barking up a brick wall. Two magic potions hadn't helped me. What a mistake they were. He is into Delia, and thinks of me as a sister, and what else is there to say about it?

"I should have gotten the cherry cheesecake," I said. "It's even more sinful."

"We'll order some of that when we finish this," Delia said, wiping a chunk off her chin. "Is it possible to get high on cheesecake? I think I'm totally high on it."

And then . . . I don't know how it happened. I can't explain it. Suddenly, my shoulders shook, and I started to cry.

I was totally surprised. The fork slipped from my hand, and I sobbed, loud, wracking sobs. I couldn't catch my breath. I couldn't stop my shoulders from jerking up and down. Sob after sob escaped my throat.

I turned in the booth, turned to the wall. But people had already seen me. I didn't really care. I just wanted to stop crying. I'm not the kind of person who goes out of control, and I *hated* it.

I felt an arm around my shoulders. I hadn't realized that Delia had slid in beside me. She hugged me tight, and as I turned, I saw that she was crying, too.

Tears burned my eyes. I choked, trying to breathe. We held on to each other and cried. We'd seen so much horror, so much death in the past few weeks.

I didn't cry at Annalee's funeral. I forced it back. I bit my lips and forced my tears back. I kept telling myself I didn't like her.

I *didn't* like Annalee. But what happened to her was horrifying and wrong. Still, I wasn't going to cry at her funeral.

And then my whole body trembled and I couldn't stop shaking at the sight of her parents standing over her grave, both of them wailing at the top of their lungs, tossing their hands above their heads and wailing, wailing out their grief.

And now all the horror was coming out. I couldn't hold it inside. All my fright, all the hideous things I'd seen, the people dead, young people . . . All too horrible to understand.

And there I was squeezed beside Delia in the red vinyl booth, the half-eaten hunk of cheesecake in front of me, sobbing, struggling to stop, sobbing, painful, wrenching sobs.

"It . . . was supposed to be me," I whispered. "Not Annalee. It was supposed to be me. My neck. My head. It could have been, Delia. It was supposed to be me."

I swallowed hard, swallowed again, trying to get control. My cheeks were hot and soaking wet from tears. My throat ached from crying.

I suddenly realized someone stood at our booth. I gazed

up to see the waitress standing there, hands clasped in front of her.

"Is something wrong with the cheesecake?" she asked.

Delia started to laugh. Soft at first but then a high, trilling laugh. And I couldn't help myself. I joined in. It was so absurd.

Something wrong with the cheesecake?

The laughter rose up from deep in my chest. And now, Delia and I were holding on to each other, laughing and laughing until more tears rolled down our faces.

The waitress stood watching us, her lips pressed together, a stern expression on her face. She was a big girl, short blond hair, small eyes close together on a round, not-pretty face. Her uniform was tight around the middle. She'd probably been sampling a lot of cheesecake.

She didn't get the joke. And she probably thought we were *really* high, not just on cheesecake.

I think she was ready to call the manager or throw us out or something. I didn't blame her. We were crying and laughing at the same time, acting like total nuts.

Ross Harper slid into the booth across from us. I hadn't seen him since his pool party. Startled, Delia and I both stopped our insane laughter.

"What's the joke?" Ross asked, settling into the booth. "Let me in on it. Must be a pretty good one."

"There's no joke. Really," I said, wiping my wet cheeks with a napkin.

The waitress turned to Ross. "Get you anything, sir?"

He glanced down at our half-eaten cheesecake slices. "No thanks. Just some sparkling water."

She gave us a final stern look, then walked off to get the water.

Ross picked up Delia's fork and sliced up a chunk of her cheesecake. "Do you mind?" He started chewing it before she could answer. "You should have gotten the Rocky Road."

"We didn't know you were coming," Delia said. "We would have ordered your favorite."

Ross took another bite. "I heard your horror film is history. Over."

"Like my movie career," I said, sighing. "That didn't last long, did it?"

"Shut up," Delia said. "You're talented. You'll get other parts."

"Maybe in a movie where everyone doesn't die," I said.

She shoved me toward the wall. We were sitting practically on top of each other.

Mopping my wet eyes with the napkin, I turned to Ross. "You weren't at Annalee's funeral."

He swallowed. "I couldn't. My dad took us all up to Sonoma. On a wine-tasting thing."

My mouth dropped open. "Seriously? Your dad goes on those touristy wine tours?"

Ross took the last bite of Delia's cheesecake. "You're joking, right? This was with the owner of the winery. He took us to this private dining room where they have all these secret reserve wines no one ever gets to drink. You know my dad. He wouldn't go unless it was top-of-the-line high-class. Then he can brag to all his douchebag friends."

"And he let you drink wine, too?" I asked.

"Are you *kidding*? He let my little sister drink. Amy is only ten." Ross snickered. "She threw up in the car." He slid my plate in front of him. "Why were you two laughing so hard?"

"Because we're crazy," Delia said.

He nodded. "I know. Everyone knows that."

"We've been kind of . . . messed up," I said. "The whole thing with the movie. It was horrible."

"Now it's over, right?" He started in on my slice.

I nodded. "My parents and Jake's parents . . . everyone decided to stop the movie. The police are all over the studio. FBI, too."

"They're talking like it could be murder," Delia said. "Like someone deliberately caused the accidents."

Ross set down his fork. "For real?"

"How else can you explain what happened?" Delia said. "You don't believe in the Curse of Mayhem Manor, do you? It had to be some sick creep murdering us one by one just like it happened in the first movie."

"Whoa." Ross lowered his eyes to the table. "Whoa. And you two could have been next."

A long silence followed. I mean, what can you say?

Finally, Ross sat up straight and stretched. He swept a hand back through his hair. "Claire, is your party still on?"

I nodded. "Still on."

"And it's still at the studio?"

"My parents insisted," I said. "They say they want me to have the biggest birthday party in history. You're coming, right?"

"For sure. Wouldn't miss it." He glanced at his phone. "But you're not having it at Mayhem Manor, are you?"

"No way," I said. "No one is going near that horrible old place. I promise."

Ross started in on my cheesecake again. Delia was texting someone on her phone. My cheeks itched from all the tears. I knew I must look awful. I slid out of the booth. "Be right back."

Ross nodded, happily pigging out.

I gazed around till I saw the sign for the restrooms. I followed it down a long, narrow hall. I could see the ladies' room at the back.

I edged to the side when I saw someone walking toward me. He came really close before I recognized him.

Puckerman.

His black hair poked out in all directions on his head. He wore a tight, sleeveless t-shirt that revealed the curly black hair on his chest and his arms. His hands were tucked into the pockets of his baggy pants.

He grinned up at me. "Hi, Claire."

I gasped. "What are *you* doing here?" My voice came out a choked whisper.

The smile faded beneath his thick beard. "Thanks for coming to Mayhem Manor the other night. You passed the test."

"So you *were* there!" I cried. "Why—?"

"Don't ask questions. We haven't finished our movie," he said in a low growl. Then I saw a flash of gray. It took me a few seconds to realize he had sprinkled something on me. On my hair. A powder. A fine gray powder.

"What *is* that? What did you just do?"

"Claire, it's an invitation. A dose of my summoning potion. It will bring you to me."

"But—but—Bring me to you *when*?"

"On Midsummer Night's eve, of course."

"No. No way. You can't—"

"You can't escape. We have to finish the film—*don't* we?"

34

MIDSUMMER NIGHT

MY PARENTS WENT WILD, TURNING the studio into an awesome party-land for my big night. I think they'd do anything to make it look like a happy place again. You know. Get people laughing and oohing and ahhing and thinking they were like at Disneyland and maybe not think about the horrible deaths for one night.

Sure, there were more security guards at the gate than usual. But once you drove inside, you were overcome by dancing lights and sparkly fairy wings on all the trees and people walking around in weird Shakespeare-type costumes.

The studio had been transformed into a dream of fairies in the woods, and people floating by in glittery robes and crowns, a fantasy world of music and mist and fun.

Before the party, my parents gave me a bright-red VW Jetta. They said it was a good starter car. I wasn't expecting a car, and I went a little nuts when they handed over the key. I mean, was I a bit emotional? Maybe.

I insisted that Delia and I test it out, so she and I took a drive up into the Hollywood Hills, and I admit it—I drove like a crazy person. Those NASCAR dudes need to take lessons from *me*. Delia left wet fingerprints on the dashboard. Really.

Somehow we made it back. But whipping around the hills like it was a thrill ride, I just had the powerful, overwhelming feeling I had to break free. Ever feel like that?

For sure, I'm a little wired these days. Can you blame me?

Anyway, party night. The studio looked *amazing*. A dance floor had been built in the plaza near the exec parking lot, and by eight o'clock, kids were already dancing under moving green laser lights to a band of five or six long-haired guys in white tuxedos.

I wore a perfect white party dress Delia and I had picked out at Barneys. The skirt only came down to midthigh, but the dress was loose and just flowed, and I thought it looked very Shakespearean, in keeping with the theme of the night.

Jake and Shawn arrived early. Shawn kept following me around like he was my date for the evening. Fat chance.

I danced with him once just to get him out of the way. He was a terrible dancer. He had no sense of rhythm at all and kept clapping off the beat as he danced.

"I know these dudes who have a guitar band," he said. "I mean, like all guitars, and they play the most awesome surf rock. I mean classic. Like Dick Dale or The Surfaris. They would have been perfect for tonight. I tried to call you, but—"

"People can't dance to that stuff," I said.

He squinted at me. "You mean people really want to dance to this electro-synth-euro-pop stuff?"

I kissed him on the cheek. You know. Give him a thrill. And I hurried away.

Where was Jake? I moved through the crowd, searching for him. Outside Soundstage A, I saw Ace, in all his mutt glory, surrounded by kids. The dog was bopping around on his hind legs, hamming it up like always. He knew he was a star, and he made the most of it. No joke. He lapped up all the attention.

My mom says the dog is a better actor than half the people who work at the studio.

A girl was feeding biscuits to the cute little guy, and he kept dancing for more.

The sparkly white lights glimmered as a warm breeze shook the trees. Two beacons, the ones they use at movie premieres, sent rays of light high in the sky. A spotlight was aimed at a movie marquee, which proclaimed: SWEET SEVEN-TEEN, STARRING CLAIRE WOODLAWN in bold black letters.

Other spotlights poured white circles of light over the crowds of kids. It was brighter than daylight. Unreal. Two bearded elves in dark tights and leafy tops ran by. And a woman with wide rhinestone-sparkly wings appeared to float along the exec cottages.

It really is *like a dream*, I thought.

Like being in a distant land. Or maybe in the Shake-speare play, all a fantasy with strange creatures floating and flying. Magic.

Two more elves scampered by. And a tall bear-creature carrying one of those shepherd hooks. A ska band was play-ing outside the commissary. Kids were lined up to get inside for food. I saw another line at a taco truck set up at the side of the building.

No sign of Jake.

I hung out with friends from school. I danced with some guys I knew. I had a slice of pizza and a few tacos and a lot of other junk. A million kisses and hugs and birthday wishes.

I guess hours went by. I kind of lost track of the time. That's how good the party was.

But then . . . then . . .

How did we decide to go to Mayhem Manor?

It's all kind of a blur. It was like the strings of twinkling lights and the music and the voices rocked my brain. Every-thing became a white, bright blur, shimmering and shaking in my head.

I actually think it was my idea. Yes. Really. I think it was.

Shawn and Jake came bopping up to me. I was dancing with a guy from school. Jake stepped between us and pulled me aside. "I've been looking for you," he said.

"Really?" That brought a smile to my face. "I've been looking for you, too."

"This dude sold me a cooler of Rolling Rock," Shawn in-terrupted. "We can't let it go to waste, right?"

"How did he get it through security?" I asked.

My parents wanted everything to go perfectly smooth tonight, so they didn't want anyone drinking. They were playing it more careful than ever. The security guards were told to take away anything that looked suspicious.

"We've got to find a place where no one will get in our faces," Shawn said. "Then we can par-tee." He glanced around. "Where can we go?"

I stared at him. "How about Mayhem Manor?" I said.

Where did the idea come from? I didn't even think about it. I felt pulled there, as if I'd been summoned. Weird.

"Huh?" Jake squinted at me. "You really want to go there? I don't believe it."

"Believe it," I said. "I feel . . . I feel . . . like I *have* to be there tonight." I flashed Jake a smile. "Like . . . it's *calling* to me."

Delia looked unhappy. She said something in my ear. I couldn't hear her. "Nothing bad can happen on my birthday," I told her. I turned to Jake. "Maybe I'll get my birthday wish tonight." *Hint, hint.*

"Maybe," he said. I could see he had no clue what I was talking about.

"Let's go," I said.

Shawn disappeared behind the taco truck and returned carrying a Styrofoam cooler. The four of us made our way to the back lot, where all the twinkling lights stopped.

The air grew way colder. We were moving through darkness now, the party far behind us. I thought there might be security guards, but I didn't see any.

I could feel my excitement rising as we tore down the yellow police tape at the front of the old mansion. I felt totally pumped. I felt giddy. I felt *crazy*.

I tried the door.

It opened easily. So dark and cold inside. I slid my hand along the wall until I clicked on ceiling lights in the front entryway.

And there we were. The four of us inside the old mansion. The scene of so much horror. But tonight, just a celebration.

I slid my hand under Jake's arm and led the way toward the front room. Suddenly, I had an idea. A crazy thought that popped into my head from out of nowhere.

I let go of Jake and spun back to the front door. "I'll be right back," I said. "Save me a beer."

And then I took off, trotting to the door, my party dress swirling around me as I ran.

I heard Delia start after me. "Claire?" she shouted. "Where are you going? Claire? Come back!"

I burst through the open door and kept running.

35

MAGIC TIME

WHY DID I SUGGEST WE BREAK in to Mayhem Manor? That's the *last* place I wanted to be. I didn't even think before I heard the words spilling from my mouth.

Go to Mayhem Manor? Really? It was as if someone had cast a spell on me, had *forced* me to go back there.

And then I had *another* bad idea. So bad it was good.

The magic of the whole night, the whole dreamy movie studio setting had washed over my brain. The lights, the elves and other creatures darting through the crowd, the fairies floating in the trees. It was my fantasy night, a night *anything* could happen.

And as I ran out of the old mansion and back into the sparkly fairyland filled with loud music and laughing voices, I had the feeling I could get one more wish. I could make one more impossible thing happen before my party ended and the real world came crashing down over me again.

Crazy. Claire, you're seriously MENTAL!

That's what part of me said. But the other part said, *Go for it!*

And there I was, running through the crowd, waving to some kids coming out of the commissary, dodging around a guy swinging a big guitar case over his shoulder, stopping while an elf darted in front of me, carrying a slice of pizza on a plate.

I made my way past the executive cottages. The lights were still brighter than day, but there weren't many people. Not much happening back here. And a few seconds later, the wardrobe building rose up at the end of the street.

My heart started to beat a little faster, and I had a tingly feeling all over my body. *It has to be here,* I told myself. *Tonight, it has to be here.*

Holding my breath, I turned and made my way to the side of the wardrobe building. And, *yes*, there it was. Puckerman's trailer. The trailer of magic potions. A bright light on in the small window.

Yes! I was counting on the magic of the night. Counting that the magic would spread itself everywhere. I know I wasn't thinking clearly. I wasn't trying to think at all. I was driven by a hunch, a brain wave from I-don't-know-where.

I ran to the trailer and climbed the steps. I pulled open the door. I stumbled inside—and *there they were!*

The shelves from floor to ceiling. The shelves filled with colorful little jars and bottles. All of the potions, Puckerman's precious potions, all magically here again.

"I knew it!" I screamed the words out loud.

No sign of the little hair ball.

I rushed up to the shelf in front of me and struggled to focus on the tiny bottles. I knew what I wanted. I remembered the color. But my eyes were watered over, from excitement, I guess. And there were no labels.

I ran my hand along the little bottles. Red liquid . . . yellow powder . . .

I knew I had to be careful. No hate potion tonight. No aging potion. Oh, no. Not tonight.

"Yes!" Finally, I found the right one. I wrapped my fingers tightly around the bottle. The powdery substance sparkled inside the glass.

The love potion. I had it in my hand. All I had to do now was sprinkle it over Jake. I had to sprinkle it on Jake and make sure I was the first person he saw. Then he would fall in love with me.

My birthday wish.

It would come true. I would *make* it come true.

I'm not crazy. I'm a smart person. Ask anyone at Beverly Hills Academy. Ask my parents or my friends. They'll tell you I'm a smart, rational person.

But tonight I believed. Tonight I believed in the magic of this crazy place, this crazy night.

I tucked the potion bottle into the canvas bag I carried everywhere. Then I spun out of the trailer and closed the door behind me. I began to jog. I saw eight or nine kids exploring the costume racks in the wardrobe building.

I turned my head so they wouldn't see me. I didn't want to be stopped. Mayhem Manor was calling to me. I wanted to get back there and work the love potion magic on Jake.

The lights were as bright as spotlights all along the studio street. I tried to stay in the shadows along the curb. Two rappers were onstage across from the commissary, shouting and gesturing, bending and pacing in front of their band. The music bounced off the trees and the soundstage wall. I felt surrounded by it. Surrounded by voices and shouts and people calling to me.

"Claire, what's up?"

"Are you going to dance?"

"Claire, is there a cake? Where are you going?"

"Yo, Claire—awesome party!"

I moved along the side of the crowd, clutching the canvas bag tightly. A security guy was watching me as I reached the back lot. I knew I couldn't let him see where I was going. The old mansion was strictly off-limits to everyone tonight.

Luckily, his phone beeped and he turned to take the call. I darted past him into the darkness of the trees. The twinkling fairy lights ended at the back lot. The dark towers of the old house rose in front of me, black against the purple sky.

I stepped over the yellow crime-scene tape and made my way to the front door. Someone had left it wide open, and I slipped inside.

From the dimly lit entryway, I could see Jake in the big front room. He had his back to me. He was talking to Delia.

Jake had a beer bottle in one hand. He kept gesturing with it.

I crept into the room. Shawn was in a corner, tilting a Rolling Rock to his mouth. And I saw Ace, standing on two legs, dancing in front of Shawn. Where was the dog's trainer? How did Ace get in the house?

No time to think about that.

My friends had started a fire. The flames crackled and danced high in the wide stone fireplace.

A fire in June? It made shadows stretch eerily over the floor.

They didn't see me. My heart started to pound as I stepped silently, silently on tiptoes behind Jake. I couldn't breathe. I felt like paralyzed by . . . what? By excitement? Paralyzed by the thought of what I was about to do?

I pulled the bottle from my bag, uncapped it, raised it. The sparkling powder inside dazzled my eyes. I raised it higher . . . higher . . . over Jake's head.

My hand trembled as I tilted the bottle and started to sprinkle the powder over his hair.

And then I let out a scream. "Oh my god! Oh no! Noooooo!"

36

"CAN I HEAR YOU SCREAM?"

I SCREAMED AS A POWERFUL blast of wind carried the glittery flakes into the air. To my horror, I realized I'd left the front door open. And now I watched the glittery powder sail up toward the ceiling.

The tiny flakes caught the flickering light of the fire and sparkled as they flew up to the dark wood rafters. And then . . . floated down, down over Delia.

Not Jake. No. Not Jake.

I watched the powder drift down over Delia, her hair, her shoulders. I cupped my hand over my mouth as I saw who my friend was staring at, staring at now with a totally love-sick expression.

Delia stared at Ace, the dog.

A strange smile spread over her face as she bent to lift the dog off the floor. She wrapped him in her arms and held him close. And then she lowered her face and kissed the mutt passionately on the tip of his snout.

Delia doesn't like dogs.

That was my insane thought as I watched her nuzzling the animal, holding him close. She began rocking him in her arms.

What have I done?

That was my second thought. I jammed the love potion bottle back into my bag.

Jake and Shawn turned to stare in shock at Delia. They knew how she felt about dogs.

"Dee, what's up?" Jake called to her, grinning. "You have a new boyfriend?"

"Isn't he the most precious thing?" Delia kissed Ace again, a slobbery wet kiss.

I lurched toward her. I wanted to explain. To apologize. But I didn't get very far. I heard a throat being cleared loudly. The click of footsteps on the hardwood floor.

I spun around. We all did. I uttered a gasp.

Puckerman stepped forward, an evil grin spread across his bearded face. He raised his hands, as if in triumph, and shouted, "Places. Places, everyone!"

No one moved. I heard the dog whimper. A heavy silence fell over the room.

"What do you want?" The words burst from my throat in a shrill, trembling question. "What are you doing here?"

"We need to finish my film now," Puckerman said. He rubbed his beard. "We've waited so long. So many years. And now it's time for a wrap. Time to finish what we started."

"What do you mean?" I cried.

"Since when is it *your* film?" Jake shouted.

"What do you *mean* finish the film?" I said. "The film is dead. It's—"

He raised a hand to silence me. His hands were so hairy, they looked like animal paws.

"Our film is not complete," Puckerman said. "Didn't you read the script? We need four more deaths." His gaze swept around the room. "How lucky there are four of you."

"Are you for *real*?" Delia cried. "This is a birthday party. Who invited *you*?"

"Let's get out of here!" Shawn said. He tossed down his beer bottle and trotted to the front door. Holding Ace tightly in her arms, Delia followed him.

Jake and I stayed back, our eyes on Puckerman.

At the front of the house, I heard Shawn pounding his fists on the heavy front door. It had been wide open when I arrived. Wide open to let in that blast of wind. But now it was closed.

"Places! Places, actors!" Puckerman shouted. "This is a closed set. The doors cannot be opened. Come back. Places! Places, everyone!"

Delia and Shawn came running back in. "He—he's crazy!" Delia stammered. "He has us locked in here. What are we going to do?"

She nuzzled the dog and made cooing sounds to him. The dog licked her face.

I've ruined everything, I told myself. *Why did I suggest we come here?*

Puckerman grinned, enjoying everyone's fear.

"He's crazy," Jake whispered to me. "Totally sick."

"Places, everyone!" Puckerman shouted. "We need to film the next scene."

He locked his eyes on me. "I believe the next scene is yours, Claire. You were supposed to have the stairway scene, but there was a mix-up."

"No. Please—" I cried. I backed against the wall. "Please—" I pictured Annalee's head gazing out blankly on the step, her neck broken, dead with a sudden *snap*.

"Since you're the birthday girl," Puckerman said, eyes flashing wildly, "you can go first. You know I've been planning this for you. I have an even better scene for you."

"Let us go!" Delia cried.

Shawn stepped up beside her. "Let us out of here, you freak!"

Puckerman bounced excitedly on his shoes. He pointed to the wall behind us. "See the camera? It's already rolling. You're all going to be stars. *Horror movie* stars. Ha-ha."

He held a hairy paw up to one ear. "Can I hear you scream now? Make it real. Because the four of you are really going to die. Come on, people. Can I hear you? Can I hear you scream?"

37

CLICK CLICK CLICK

"YOU—YOU'RE REALLY GOING TO *KILL* US?" I stammered. "Why? What is this about?"

He tossed back his furry head and laughed. He had the ugliest laugh I've ever heard. It sounded more like choking than laughter.

"You really don't have a clue—do you!" he said.

Beside me, Delia held Ace close to her. The dog was whimpering softly.

I gazed straight ahead at Puckerman. I couldn't breathe. I couldn't move.

"Sit down, people!" Puckerman shouted, motioning us down with both hands. "Everyone down. It's story time."

No one moved.

"NOW!" he shrieked.

We obediently dropped to the hard floor. I settled on my

knees, determined to stay alert, to watch for the first chance to escape.

He leaned against a stage light. "You're going to die, so you might as well know why," he said.

He cleared his throat again. He spit something disgusting onto the floor. "I've always had a dream," he said. "Do you have a dream? My dream was to become the greatest horror-movie director of all time. The best in movie history."

His tiny dark eyes stayed on me. I felt a chill grip the back of my neck.

"When they built Mayhem Manor," he continued, "I saw my big opportunity. Oh, yes. Oh, yes. I used my potions to get what I wanted. I got them to name me director of the film. No problem. And then I was set to make my mark on movie history. Because I planned to make a horror movie in which all the actors *actually died.*"

"You're crazy!" Jake shouted. He started to his feet, but I pulled him back down.

"Jake, he'll *kill* you," I whispered.

Puckerman shook his head. "The greatest horror-movie idea in history, and they stopped me. After only three murders—three *delicious* murders—they shut down my film. The idiots! Idiots!"

He IS crazy, I thought. *He directed the film in 1960, and he deliberately killed those actors. Those three deaths weren't accidents. They were murders.* And then I realized: *He's crazy enough to kill us all.*

"How angry was I?" he screamed. "How angry? Angry

enough to stay alive. I'm 112, but my potions kept me alive. I stayed alive all these years to await my chance."

Puckerman paced back and forth in front of us. "All these years, I waited in this house for a new cast to arrive. Waited. Waited patiently. And then, there you were. Sixty years later, time to start the film again."

An ugly grin spread on his hairy face. "And what wonderful scenes we shot. Lana with her lovely hand on the table. Jeremy's pretty face in the microwave. Oh yes. I was there in his dressing room. I rigged the microwave and filmed the whole wonderful scene. And then . . . Annalee doing such a beautiful fall. What a trouper!" He laughed his ugly laugh.

"But, my dear actors, tonight will be our triumph, our greatest night. We have four more scenes to shoot, one for each of you. This is so exciting. Tonight we finish my masterpiece, *Mayhem Manor*."

"No way!" Shawn cried. "We're not cooperating. We won't do this."

"Of course you will," Puckerman said softly. "You want to be *stars*, don't you?"

He waved a hairy paw at me. "Come up here, birthday girl. I summoned you here because it's your special day. And so, the first scene is yours. Are you ready for the grandfather clock scene?"

I swallowed. I raised myself to my feet on trembling legs. I didn't want to step forward. But I didn't seem to be in control. He had used some kind of potion on me.

"Wh-what's the grandfather clock scene?" I stammered, my throat too choked to make a sound above a whisper.

He pointed to the tall wood-and-glass clock in the corner. "You walk over there. You try to stop the clock. You don't realize the pendulum has been sharpened until it can cut through steel. You grab for the pendulum as it swings. You grab for it with both hands. Slice slice. The blades cut fast. You scream. The blood spurts up. In your shock, you fall forward—and slice your whole body to slivers." He giggled.

"Nooo!" A wail escaped my throat. "You wouldn't. You won't. You—"

"Come on, Claire. This is your close-up, your moment in movie history. You won't let a little pain stand in your way—will you?"

"No. Please. Please."

"The camera is rolling. Step forward, Claire. I'm sure you can do this scene in one take."

I turned to my friends. Why weren't they helping me? Shawn sat by himself in the corner. Delia held the dog in her lap and stared straight ahead. Jake gazed up at me but didn't move.

Were they all under spells?

I couldn't stop myself. I felt *pulled* to the tall, old clock. One foot, then the other. I could see the long silvery pendulum inside the tall glass door, swinging from side to side, making a loud *click* with each swing.

Click. Click. Click.

Counting off the seconds before my painful death.

"Go ahead, Claire," Puckerman urged, walking close behind me. "The clock is driving you crazy. You want to stop it so you can think straight. Go ahead. Grab the door handle. Pull it open—and reach for the pendulum with both hands."

My breath caught in my throat. I could feel the blood pulsing at my temples.

I wanted to scream. I wanted to run. But I couldn't stop myself.

Click. Click. Click.

I grabbed the handle on the side of the glass—and pulled open the door.

38

THE DIRECTOR'S CUT

CLICK. CLICK. CLICK.

I held the glass door of the clock open and stared at the shiny pendulum as it swung back and forth. As if hypnotized, I couldn't take my eyes off it as I stood trembling, not breathing, imagining... imagining the unbearable pain of having my hands chopped up... sliced and bleeding... and then my whole body cut.

Click. Click. Click.

"Go ahead, Claire." Puckerman's voice broke into my panic. "Reach for it. This is your moment. Reach for it."

I raised my hands in front of me. I curled my fingers, preparing to grab the sharpened metal.

Click. Click. Click.

"Go for it, Claire." The evil bearded creature forcing me, willing me with his mind... his twisted mind.

My hands slid forward. I couldn't stop them. I had no control.

"Not like that. Like *this*," Puckerman instructed. "Grab it. Grab it."

He coiled his hairy paws, demonstrating. He moved toward me, eyes on my hands. "Grab it."

"No," I uttered. I lurched back.

I bumped Puckerman. He stumbled over my leg—and toppled forward.

He shot out both hands, trying to stop his fall. But he had nothing to grab on to.

"Whoooa." His cry was cut off as the top of his head hit the clock.

Click click.

I gasped as the pendulum blade sliced off his head. A fast, clean cut.

The little man's body crumpled like a balloon deflating, and his head bounced on the floor in front of me. It rolled a few feet, then stopped, nesting in its own thick beard.

The dark eyes remained open, staring blankly up at me, still bulging with surprise.

"Wow! Oh, wow!" I heard Shawn cry out behind me. "We're going to be okay!"

Jake came up behind me and put his hands on my trembling shoulders. "Claire? You're all right?"

I couldn't stop shaking. I stared down in horror at Puckerman's head. And then I choked out, "No blood." I pointed frantically. "Look. He didn't bleed. There's no blood."

"What a freak!" Shawn declared. "Let's get out of here."

I turned and saw Delia standing up now, a big smile on her face. She held Ace in her arms and kept nuzzling him and pressing him against her.

Shawn grabbed up two beer bottles and pumped them over his head. He did a victory dance around Delia, shouting and laughing.

Jake tugged my hand. "Come on, Claire. Let's get away from this place. Let's find a way out of here."

I forced myself to stop looking at Puckerman's sliced-up head, his bloodless body heaped on the floor. I started to breathe normally. I forced my heartbeats to slow.

"Yes," I said to Jake. "Yes, let's get out of here. We're okay. Let's go."

The four of us started to the front door.

But then a hoarse voice rang out behind us. *"Not so fast! Where do you think you're going? We still have scenes to shoot."*

I gasped and spun around. And stared down at Puckerman's head on the floor.

The fat eyebrows moved. The dark eyes blinked. The lips tightened around the teeth.

"The door is still locked," Puckerman's head shouted. "One little accident won't stop my movie. Places! Places, everyone!"

39

TIME TO DANCE?

I FELT MY HEARTBEATS PULSE IN MY CHEST. I struggled to breathe.

The head—the ugly, bearded head—it shouted at us.

And then we all screamed as Puckerman's stumpy body pulled itself up. It staggered forward, bent, and lifted the head off the floor, lifted it to its place on the creature's hairy shoulders.

The hands twisted the head on the neck, twisted it right, then left, and pressed it down.

"There. That's better," Puckerman said, moving his head from side to side with both hands, testing it.

He turned to me. "That was good improvising, Claire. I got it all on film. See? We are making progress."

I stared at him with my mouth hanging open. I couldn't breathe. I couldn't speak.

"What's wrong?" he asked. "Aren't you glad to see me

back? Did you really think I waited sixty years to fail because of a minor accident?" He giggled.

He moved forward suddenly and tightened his fingers around my arm. "Come on, Claire. It's getting late. The camera is rolling." He started to pull me toward the kitchen door.

"Let go!" I cried. "What are you doing? Where are you taking me?"

He glared at the others, daring them to try to help me. "Let's hurry. We have four deaths to go."

"No! Let go!" I tried to pull free of his grasp, but the little beast had inhuman strength. He pulled me into the kitchen. I saw the others follow, their faces tight with fear.

"Let go!" I screamed again. "What are you going to do?"

"Let's do the toaster scene," he said in my ear. "Your turn, Claire. No tricks this time. Are you a good dancer? I know you're going to be terrific."

He pushed me to the counter in front of the toaster, gleaming in the dim light. "Go ahead. Do it, Claire," he urged, pushing my arm from behind. "Pick it up. Hurry. Pick it up. It's your turn to dance."

40

"THAT'S A WRAP"

MY HAND TREMBLED OVER THE TOASTER. I could feel the blood racing at my temples. Behind me, my friends were pleading with Puckerman to let me go.

He whipped around furiously and menaced them with his fists. "Don't worry. Your turn will come."

He gave me a hard shove from behind. "Go ahead. Pick up the toaster. Now."

When he turned back to threaten my friends, I had a few seconds to act. I reached into my bag, the bag I kept the stolen potions in. I grabbed the love potion and pulled it out.

I had a desperate plan. Pour the love potion on Puckerman. He instantly falls in love with me. And it makes him change his mind. He loves me too much to kill me with the toaster.

Yes, it was a crazy, desperate plan. But I couldn't think of anything else.

"Grab the toaster," Puckerman said, with another shove. "Let's see you dance."

"I don't think so," I said. I spun around, raised the potion bottle over his head, and dumped the glittery powder onto his thick, matted hair.

"Hey—!" The little creep uttered a startled cry. He slapped at his hair, trying to brush the powdery flakes away. "What did you do? What was that, Claire? What did you do?"

He staggered back against the counter. He glared at me furiously.

Where was the love in his eyes?

As I stared back at him, his eyes grew watery. The color seemed to wash from his face. His dark beard, his bushy hair faded to gray, then white. His face sagged and wrinkled. His stumpy body hunched over, sank to the floor. A weak moan escaped his throat.

"Oh, wow," I murmured, moving to join my friends. I knew what I'd done. I'd grabbed the wrong potion. Again. I'd grabbed the *aging* potion from my bag.

I tossed the bottle to the floor. I was panting hard, struggling to catch my breath. My fear made my whole body shudder.

I felt Jake step up behind me and put his hands on my shoulders. He held me tight. "It's okay," he whispered. "Look. It's okay."

As the four of us stared in disbelief, Puckerman aged before our eyes. His skin began to peel off. Gray bone showed through open patches in his face. The skin drooped, then oozed off his head, revealing the toothy skeleton under-neath. His body shrank into his baggy overalls.

Puckerman slumped in a heap on the kitchen floor, a pile of wrinkled, decayed skin, dried-up organs, and yellowed bones. And then the bones and skin disintegrated, just fell apart, crumbling to a pile of gray ashes.

A pile of dry ashes at our feet.

"We're outta here!" Shawn cried, and took off toward the front.

"This movie is over!" I shouted. "That's a wrap!"

Laughing like lunatics, shouting out our victory at the top of our lungs, we ran to the front door.

41

THE FINAL CURTAIN

WE HAD THE PREMIERE OF *Mayhem Manor* at Century City.

I know, I know. How could there be a premiere of a film that was never finished?

Well, the cameras were rolling the whole time, remember?

They captured Puckerman's head being sliced off in the clock. And then his body pulling the head back on. We also had Puckerman's amazing transformation into an old man— and then to *dust.*

My parents gave Les Bachman the go-ahead. And he turned the whole thing into a wild, insane horror movie/ documentary.

Jake, Shawn, Delia, and I sat halfway back in the theater so we could see the premiere audience's reaction. We didn't have to guess. They were *loving* it. They screamed and hid their eyes at the horrible deaths. And you should have heard them laughing their heads off when Delia started kissing the dog near the end.

Don't worry. Delia is fine now. That spell wore off quickly. Now, she and Shawn have a thing going. Delia is a happy person. Not to mention a movie star.

And me? Sure, there were a lot of horrifying moments. I'll never forget that people died. But I can't tell you how exciting it was to see myself on that big screen in front of hundreds of people. They cheered when I poured the potion on Puckerman's head and he started to grow old and shrink. I guess I'm the hero in the film.

As we followed the crowd out of the theater, I felt an arm go around my shoulder.

I turned my head and saw that it was Jake. He spun me around and hugged me. "Claire, you were awesome," he said.

"Hey, thanks," I said.

"I never told you," he continued. "But when we were trapped in the house with that psycho, I . . . well . . . I was so scared for you. I . . . I didn't know what to do."

I could feel my heart beating. I held on tightly. I didn't want the hug to end. I pressed my face against his. I just wanted to stay like this.

"I'm glad you're okay," Jake said softly.

The love potion, I thought. *I still have it in my bag.*

Jake kept his arm around me as we followed Shawn and Delia out the door.

We both sighed and raised our faces to the sky as we

stepped into the night air. The air smelled so fresh and sweet. All around us, people were talking about the movie. Smiling at me. Congratulating me.

Magic.

A magical night.

I couldn't resist. I had to try it. After everything that had happened . . . why not?

I raised the little bottle—and poured some sparkly love potion crystals on Jake's head.

He turned and looked at me. He smiled. He wrapped his arm around my waist and pulled me close. "Hey, babe," he said, "what was *that*?"

If we shadows have offended,
Think but this, and all is mended,
That you have but slumbered here
While these visions did appear.
And this weak and idle theme,
No more yielding, but a dream . . .

—William Shakespeare,
A Midsummer Night's Dream

GOFISH

R.L. STINE

What did you want to be when you grew up?
I wanted to be a cartoonist and draw comic books. But I quickly discovered I had no drawing talent whatsoever.

Were you a reader or a non-reader growing up?
At first, I read only comic books. Then I discovered sci-fi stories by Ray Bradbury. I started reading all the sci-fi stories I could find.

When did you realize you wanted to be a writer?
When I was nine. I'd stay in my room typing stories and joke magazines. I never wanted to go outside and play. I was a weird kid.

What's your most embarrassing childhood memory?
Throwing up on the school bus. I was in second grade. I heaved right down the aisle. They had to send for a new bus.

What's your favorite childhood memory?
Going fishing with bamboo poles in a river with my dad. He never had much time to spend with us kids. The fishing days were special, even though we never caught anything.

As a young person, who did you look up to most?
The cartoonists who did *MAD* comics and all the EC Horror Comics. I thought they were brilliant and pored over their work like someone viewing masterpieces in a museum.

What was your favorite thing about school?
I wasn't much of a student. I was bored in school. I wanted to be home, writing stories and drawing comics.

What was your least favorite thing about school?
Gym class. I was terrible in all sports. I dreaded gym class every time.

What were your hobbies as a kid? What are your hobbies now?
I don't have time for hobbies. But remember, I live in New York City. The city is a wonderful, exciting show. You only need hobbies if you live somewhere else.

What was your first job, and what was your "worst" job?
My first job when I arrived in NYC was writing for six movie fan magazines. I made up interviews with the stars all day long. I never actually interviewed anyone. I just made it all up. Very creative work.

What book is on your nightstand now?
Wolf Hall by Hilary Mantel.

How did you celebrate publishing your first book?
My first book was called *How to Be Funny*. I had a big book signing in the old Doubleday bookstore on Fifth Avenue. And NO ONE came. No one had ever heard of me. It wasn't much of a celebration.

Where do you write your books?
In my apartment. I have an office I share with a skeleton, several dummies, and my dog.

What challenges do you face in the writing process, and how do you overcome them?
My main challenge is how to be scary for kids without being *too* scary. I solve it by using a lot of teasing and humor in the books to lighten things up.

Which of your characters is most like you?
None, I hope.

What makes you laugh out loud?
Laurel & Hardy films. I can watch the same one ten times and still laugh just as hard. I have a very large library of L & H films.

What do you do on a rainy day?
Write, of course.

What's your idea of fun?
I love hanging out with my wife, my son, and his wife. I love going on beach vacations. I love crowded insane places like Disney World and Atlantis in the Bahamas.

What's your favorite song?
"Skylark." It's by Johnny Mercer and Hoagy Carmichael.

Who is your favorite fictional character?
Bertie Wooster and Jeeves in the P.G. Wodehouse novels. I'm a Wodehouse fanatic.

If you could travel in time, where would you go and what would you do?
I would love to go back to NYC in the 1880s. It was portrayed so romantically in Jack Finney's book, *Time and Again*. It was a great, exciting time in the city. For example: There were twice as many theaters in New York in 1880 as there are today.

What's the best advice you have ever received about writing?
Keep it as simple as possible.

Do you ever get writer's block? What do you do to get back on track?
I don't have time for writer's block. Too many books to write! I do a tremendous amount of planning and outlining before I sit down to write. That makes it nearly impossible to have writer's block.

What do you want readers to remember about your books?
I want them to remember that they were overall entertaining and fun, and made reading a fun experience.

What do you consider to be your greatest accomplishment?
Terrifying several generations of kids. Also: encouraging millions of kids to discover the joy of reading.

What would your readers be most surprised to learn about you?
That I love opera and ballet (and country music).

SQUARE FISH